T0088066

LOVE
BETWEEN MEN

SEDUCTIVE STORIES OF
AFTERNOON PLEASURES

EDITED BY
SHANE ALLISON

CLEiS
PRESS

Published in the United States by Cleis Press, Inc., 2246 Sixth Street, Berkeley, CA 94710.

Printed in the United States.
Cover design: Scott Idleman/Blink
Cover photograph: Celesta Danger
Text design: Frank Wiedemann

First Edition.
10 9 8 7 6 5 4 3 2 1

Trade paper ISBN: 978-1-62778-039-1
E-book ISBN: 978-1-62778-056-8

Contents

INTRODUCTION: SEX IS A COCK RING-CLAD ANGEL

The night Rashaan proposed to me, I cried like a sappy soap opera diva. He popped the question right after dessert at our favorite bar-and-grille haunt where the buffalo wings will make you want to slap your mama. There he was on bended knee, asking me to marry him as he slipped the ring on my plump digit. Heads turned. Thunderous claps erupted throughout the restaurant while some mean-mugged with disapproval, but most smiled with congratulatory expressions across their faces. I was happier than Oprah Winfrey at an all-you-can-eat barbecue buffet. That week we fucked in every room of the house: on the kitchen table, on the couch, even in the backyard after a sweaty day of lawn work.

I wake up many mornings with Rashaan's mouth on a place most private. We messed around the first night we met. It was at some shady pickup bar I normally wouldn't have been caught dead in. There were guys that offered to buy me drinks, but none of them held my interest; then Rashaan blew in. He asked if the bar stool next to me was taken, and I took one look at his tall, chocolate brawn, and said no. He had short, curly hair, faded out on the sides. Rashaan was dressed in a white, V-neck T-shirt and boot-cut jeans. I could smell his cologne even in the haze of cigarette smoke. We spoke all night through the house music that was being woven by the bar DJ. We had lots in common; the same loves and pet peeves like why there were no gay black men on "Queer as Folk." "At least Melanie's partner should have been a big, butch black chick," he said. I fell in love with his humor. A man who can make me laugh is a plus in my little black book.

We went back to his place, where we spent more time getting to know each other. I hesitated at first about whether I should accompany him, since I hardly knew him—he could be some gay serial killer!—but he had a trustworthy way about him. After a glass of cheap, liquor-store wine, we fucked until four in the morning. He asked for my number. I started to give him a fake one, but decided against it and jotted my legit digits in the palm of his hand. When I got outside of his apartment complex, my phone rang. "I just wanted to see if your number was real," he said. I laughed and told him how silly he was. Days turned into weeks, weeks into months, and we became inseparable, one of those annoying couples who hold hands as they browse vintage stores and window-shop.

I used to think love was a Tasmanian monster under my bed, much like sex is a leather-clad angel with a cock ring halo. I thought it only happened to people like Jennifer Aniston or Katherine Heigl in corny romantic comedies. There was a time when I thought I was doomed to be lonely, cursed to share myself with only glossy, horse-hung, gay porn gods with spray-on tans, not that I have issue with horse-hung. I thought that if I fell in love, it would quickly be stripped away from me like some mistakenly bestowed Purple Heart awarded to me for *hanging in there*, but it hasn't happened yet, knock on wood. This book celebrates not only the sultry sex that goes down under the sheets between the men who share their lives, but also hopeful encounters between those who continue to search tirelessly for that perfect combination of love and the perfect fuck. These stories comprise that rarest of anthologies: bedtime reading for gay couples. The talented writers I've chosen have filled each story with romance, passion and lots of lust.

Two husbears travel down South to meet up with a horned-up twink in Jeff Mann's "One Afternoon in the Bible Belt." A sneaky environmentalist is sandwiched between rock-hard dick hounds Eddy and Dale in Bob Vickery's salacious tale, "Loggers." Life partners have a Sunday morning roll in the sack in Hank Edwards's "Breakfast in Bed." Rob Rosen's "Skyrockets in Flight" is delicious, with naughty bits in every throbbing line. These are just a few of the romantic stories of male-on-male sex that grace the pages of this anthology. So lie back with the one you love or the one you lust after and enjoy. Clothing is optional.

Shane Allison
Tallahassee, Florida

LOGGERS

Bob Vickery

There's a slight breeze blowing in through the cab window, cooling off some of the sweat I've been working up. It ain't the only thing blowing. I reach up and stretch, locking my fingers together, and pull my knees wider apart. They can only go so far with my jeans down around my ankles. I look down at the back of Eddy's head, watching it twist back and forth as I fuck his mouth with long, slow strokes. "Hell, Eddy," I laugh. "I do believe you're getting bald."

Eddy stops his sucking and looks up, still holding my cock in his hand. He gives me one of his easy, good ol' boy smiles. "You should be careful what you say to me while your dick's in my mouth," he growls.

I grin. "Sorry. Didn't mean to break your stride." I scratch my beard and settle back into the truck's seat. "Go ahead. Don't let me stop you."

Eddy's blue eyes gleam. I swear, somewhere back in Eddy's family tree some great-granddaddy must have fucked a wolf, 'cause I can see the family resemblance now. He slowly runs his tongue up the length of my dickmeat, sucking gently on the head, tonguing my cum slit. It always excites the hell out of me, watching my dickmeat pump the face of a man as handsome as Eddy. Without any warning, he plunges down, swallowing all eight and a half inches. I feel the softness of Eddy's beard press down against my low-hangers. Up and down his mouth goes, his tongue wrapping around my dick, squeezing it, caressing it. Sweet Jesus, can that boy suck cock! It's one of his most endearing qualities. I look up at the cab's roof, letting the sensations sweep over me, and start giving out some mighty groans to show Eddy my appreciation.

Eddy's sucking on my balls now, first the left one, then the right, rolling each one around in his mouth, while he strokes my fuckstick slowly. He's humping his fist with the same even tempo, and I reach down to give him a helping hand. His dickmeat is slick with spit and precum and slides in and out of my hand as easy as butter on a hot skillet.

My other hand rubs and strokes across Eddy's chest, feeling those pumped-up hard pecs and the soft fur that covers them. I grab his left nipple between thumb and forefinger and squeeze hard. Eddy, his mouth full of my balls, grunts his approval, and I slap the back of his head. "Didn't your mama teach you not to talk with your mouth full?" I grin. Eddy laughs and I pull his face up to mine, shoving my tongue deep into his mouth.

Eddy rolls over on top of me, and his muscular arms wrap around me in a powerful bear hug. I feel his hard flesh pressed tight against mine, the sweaty skin sliding back and forth across my chest, his thick dick dry humping my belly. I breathe in the strong man-smell of Eddy's sweat; we've both just gotten off an eight-hour shift of logging redwoods and we reek. I work a finger into Eddy's tight bunghole with excruciating slowness, up to the third knuckle. My finger is encased in warm velvet. I wiggle it, pushing against the prostate, and Eddy goes fucking crazy, thrashing around in the cab, squirming against me, groaning loud enough to wake the dead. This boy needs a serious fucking.

Still kissing Eddy, I pull my finger out of his ass and grope in the glove compartment for a condom. I roll one down my shaft, Eddy shifts his hips up, and we resume playing dueling tongues as I slowly impale him. I fuck Eddy with short, quick thrusts, and he pumps his hips to meet me, matching me stroke for stroke. My hand's wrapped around Eddy's thick shaft, jerking him off like there's hell to pay.

Fucking in the front seat of a truck cab ain't the most comfortable way to get off. Eddy's head is bent down to keep from bumping the roof, and the stick shift keeps hitting me in the leg. But neither of us is complaining. I settle into a steady rhythm of plowing ass, Eddy's face just inches away from mine. I look deep into those wild blue eyes, and he stares back at me, his eyes narrowed in concentration, his lips pulled back into a soundless snarl. A low, half whimper comes out of his mouth and then another. I spit in my hand and continue stroking his dickmeat. The whimper turns into a long, trailing groan. I stroke faster now, and he groans again, loud. I squeeze his nipple and that does the trick. Eddy arches his back, and his body begins shuddering as he shoots his load. The first squirt gets me right in the face, just below my left eye. The next two hit me on the chin. Eddy's bellowing like a damn bull-moose, and the squirts just keep on a-cumming. I'm soaked with the stuff before he's done.

I shove my dick once more hard up its entire length into Eddy's ass and that does the trick for me. I groan loudly, and

Eddy plants his mouth roughly on top of mine. He tongues me damn well down to my throat as my jizz shoots into the condom up his ass. There's a lot of thrashing about, a lot of crashing into ashtrays and door handles, until finally, things quiet down. Eddy softly licks his cum off my face as I lie back, eyes closed, feeling the late afternoon breeze blow in through the window. I can hear the leaves outside rustling, and, farther off in the distance, the buzz of the chain saws of the afternoon shift.

After a few minutes, Eddy pushes himself up. "I gotta take a leak," he says, and climbs out of the cab. I watch him lazily, admiring his fine, tight ass, as he stands on the road edge buck naked and pisses down the hillside.

His body suddenly stiffens. "Hey, Dale," he calls over his shoulder toward me. "Come over here."

I'm almost drifting off to sleep now. "Why?" I ask irritably.

"Just get over here, goddamn it!"

Grumbling, I push out of the truck's cab and walk over to where Eddy's standing. "What's up?" I growl.

Eddy points down below and I follow the direction of his finger. Way down below I can see the work crew cutting away at the redwoods growing on the valley floor. But that's not what's got Eddy's attention. He's pointing closer up, where the logging road winds along the side of the hill before it climbs to the spot where we're standing. And now I see what's got his attention. Halfway down the ridge, by the side of the road, there's a man lying on his belly, snapping pictures of the tree-cutting operation going on below him. A backpack lies by his side.

I look at Eddy. "What do you think he's up to?" I ask.

Eddy shrugs. We watch the dude for a moment longer, not saying anything. "I bet he's a tree-hugger," Eddy finally says. I nod, keeping my eyes on him. "I think you're right." At this distance it's hard to tell, but he looks like he's not much more than a kid. I turn to Eddy, grinning. "Let's take him!"

The last few hundred feet, I switch off the engine and coast around the curve. The tree-hugger's still there, stretched out on a small patch of grass a little way off from the road, still snapping pictures. I look at Eddy and put a finger to my lips. We climb out of the truck and creep over toward him.

We get to just a few feet away from him. "What the hell do you think you're doing?" I bark.

This gets the desired effect. The guy jumps up and whirls around, facing us with wide eyes. I can see he's young, all right, early twenties maybe, clean-shaven, but with a shaggy mane of dark blond hair. His cutoffs show two powerfully muscled legs. Most likely a mountain biker, I think. I still got the picture in my head of how tight his ass looked when he was on his belly. The kid stares at us, saying nothing.

"The man asked what you're doing," Eddy says quietly, his wolf's eyes squinting. Eddy can look real mean when he wants to.

The kid swallows. "I was watching the loggers down below."

"Yeah," I say. "And taking pictures too."

The kid's eyes dart to my face, then Eddy's, then back to mine again. It's clear he wishes bad he was somewhere else. I can't help but notice how good-looking he is, with a firm jaw, alert brown eyes, tight body. "Look," he says, his voice low. "I'm just taking a hike. Photography's a hobby of mine."

I narrow my eyes, doing my best Clint Eastwood. "What's your name?"

The kid meets my gaze, and, I have to give him credit, holds it steadily. "Mark," he says.

"This is private property, Mark," I rap. "Owned by Carolina-Pacific Lumber. You got no business being here."

"Yeah, and you guys got no business cutting down those old-growth redwoods!" Mark blurts. "There's a court injunction forbidding you from doing it!"

Well, that sure as hell clears up any doubts about whether or not he's a tree-hugger. I turn to Eddy. "I think we ought to take him down to the foreman's trailer." Which is pure bluff. I have no intention turning this kid over to anyone, much less those fucking animals down below. I just want to throw a scare in him.

The low rumble of a truck comes from around the bend behind us, and me and Eddy turn to look in its direction. The kid, quick to grab the opportunity, sprints off the road and jumps down the side of the ridge, half falling, half running, until he's swallowed up by the trees. A logging truck comes around the curve, loaded down with redwoods, all old growth. Mike, the driver, toots his horn and waves, and Eddy and me wave back. We watch the truck round the next bend in a cloud of dust.

Eddy nods toward the kid's backpack. "Our buddy seems to have left something behind."

I grin. "You want to go look for him?"

Eddy gives me a disgusted look. "Are you crazy? I ain't climbing down that hill. I'm going home to a cold beer."

I'm already sliding down the hill. "You ain't going nowhere with the keys to the truck in my pocket," I call over my shoulder. "You can either wait or come with me."

Behind me, I hear Eddy curse. He starts scrambling down the hill after me.

We find Mark just a little way off, sitting on a log with his right boot and sock off. His ankle is already beginning to swell badly.

"Looks like you had a little accident," I say mildly.

Mark glares at me but says nothing.

"Come on," I say. "Me and Eddy'll get you back to the truck."

When we get to the road, Mark shakes us off like so many flies. He hobbles to his backpack and pulls out an ace bandage.

"Get in the truck," I say. "You can do that back at our place."

Mark begins wrapping the bandage around his ankle. "Just leave me alone. I can get back on my own."

"Yeah, right. It's eight miles back to the main road."

"That's my problem." Mark stands up. He takes a step and grimaces with pain.

"Don't be a jerk," I say impatiently. "Get in the damn truck."

Mark starts limping down the road. He flips me off without looking back.

I shrug. "Suit yourself." I open the truck door and climb in. I look at Eddy. "You comin' or are you walkin' too?"

Eddy glances at Mark and then climbs into the truck. I start the engine and begin pulling away.

"Wait!" Mark shouts. I stop. The kid is blushing now, and his eyes are shooting daggers at me. Damn if he don't look sexier than a motherfucker. I feel my cock stir. "You're right," he says. "There's no way I can make it back on my own." I can tell it's killing him to admit it.

I throw open the door. "Hop in."

Mark's face twitches, and, in spite of himself, he grins. "Hop is about the only thing I can do right now," he says.

Mark takes a pull from his beer. He's sitting in a chair by the fire, with his foot propped up on a stool. "What those fuckers you work for are doing is illegal, you know. Like I said, there's a court injunction against logging old growth in this area."

I give him a long, deadpan look. "What if me and Eddy told you we agree with you?"

"Yeah, right."

"We do, you know." I nod toward his camera. "Look, we could just pull the film out of your camera right now, if we wanted to. You think you could stop us?"

Mark glares at me. He's a suspicious li'l fucker, all right. "Then why were you guys out there cutting down the trees along with all your asshole friends?"

The kid is getting my goat. "Because, you little college punk," I say slowly, "if we refuse, we get our asses fired. And logging's the only thing we know how to do." I glare back at him until he finally looks away. "Eddy and me grew up in this area. Our daddies were loggers. So were our granddaddies. But this shit is new, they're clearcutting everything. They're killing the land. In twenty years there ain't going to be nothing left to log."

"Hell, man," Eddy chimes in. "If those pictures will slow the cutting down, we *want* you to get through with them."

Mark gives a short laugh. "Great. You just get me to my car tomorrow and I'll do the rest." He kills the rest of his bottle and scans the room. "You guys live here together?" he asks. I nod. I can almost hear what he's thinking, that there's only one bedroom in the place. He looks at me again, his eyes bold. "You guys lovers?"

Eddy shifts in his seat. "You ask a lot of questions," he growls.

I return his stare. "Yeah, we're lovers," I say levelly. "You got a problem with that?"

Mark shakes his head. "Not at all." He grins, and after a beat of five, adds, "As a matter of fact, I swing that way myself."

There's a long silence while me and Eddy chew on this little piece of information. I give Mark a hard steady look, trying to keep a poker face, but I can feel my heart pounding. Mark looks back at me, the firelight flickering across his young, handsome face, his eyes gleaming, his lips pulled back into an easy smile. Damn! These kids nowadays are all so sure we'll go to hell and back for a piece of their ass. The trouble is, they're right. At least when they look like Mark. My dick starts stiffening under my jeans, and I shift in my chair so as not to give Mark the satisfaction of noticing. "So what do you want me to do about that?" I grunt.

Mark's grin widens. "Oh, I don't know. Maybe we can all think of something." He pulls his T-shirt off and then slowly unzips his cutoffs and pulls them down, carefully lifting his right ankle to kick them off. He sits back in the chair again, looking at both of us with a calm expression. Even half-erect, his cock is impressive: thick, meaty, with a large, mushroom head. Firelight dances over his veined, slightly twitching dickmeat and the fleshy balls beneath it. I glance at Eddy, but his eyes are fixed with a hungry gleam on Mark's naked body. Eddy always was a pig for dick. But hell, so am I. Eddy begins rubbing his own dick under the heavy fabric of his jeans. He shoots a quizzical glance in my direction, and I nod agreement. *Yeah, Eddy, let's go for it.*

Mark sees my nod and laughs. "Hell, with my ankle like it is, I can't come to you. If this is going to happen, you guys are going to have to come over here."

I don't do nothing for a couple of beats. Don't want the kid to think I'm too eager. Finally I stand up, walk over to Mark and stand in front of him, my crotch inches from his face. "Okay, fucker," I growl. "Now what?"

Mark reaches over and slips his hand under my shirt, sliding it across my belly. His fingers hook around the top of my jeans and he draws me closer. He places his mouth over the rough fabric just above my cock and gently bites. With his other hand, Mark begins pumping his dickmeat. I reach down and squeeze his left nipple, not gently. Mark groans. He undoes my belt buckle and unzips my fly. I just stand there, letting him do all the work. He's no longer wearing that sly smile; he has an expression I know well: dick hunger, and it gets my dick granite hard knowing it's me who's put that aching look on his face. He pulls my jeans down to my knees, and then my shorts. My cock springs to full attention. I glance over toward Eddy and see he's already whipped out his own dick and is furiously beating off.

Mark reaches over and squeezes my cock gently; a little precum pearl oozes through my cum slit. Mark laps it up. "My favorite flavor," he grins, looking up at me.

"Yeah," I laugh. "Rum raisin."

Mark laughs too. He runs his tongue up the length of my dickmeat, swirls it twice around the head and then swallows it all, his nose buried deep into my pubes. My knees buckle for a second, and then, holding the kid's head with both hands, I begin fucking his mouth with long, slow strokes. Mark cups my balls with his hand and squeezes them gently.

I glance over at Eddy, still on the other side of the room, still yanking his crank, those beautiful, low-hanging balls of his just bouncing to the tempo of his beat. "Hey, Eddy!" I yell. "Get your skinny ass over here!" I look down at Mark, who's looking back up at me, my cock shoved full to the base down his throat. "Eddy's always a little shy at parties," I explain.

Eddy lurches over, his jeans down around his ankles, his thick meat swinging heavily from side to side. I pull him over to me and kiss him hard, my tongue probing deep into his mouth.

I spit in my hand and then wrap it around Eddy's dick, sliding it up and down the thick shaft. Eddy's blue wolf eyes narrow, and a small groan escapes from his mouth.

Mark begins tonguing Eddy's fleshy nut sac, sucking on one ball, then the other, then the two of them together. He pushes my hand aside and deep-throats Eddy's dick, his mouth working its way up and down the thick shaft of meat. All the time he's fucking his own fist hard and fast. It's clear that Mark's a brother dick pig as well. After a few sucks, he returns to my meat, then back to Eddy's. I look at Eddy's and my dicks thrusting out side by side. Eddy's is red, and thicker than mine, uncut and heavily veined. A good, meaty workingman's dick. Mine is longer and darker, cut, with a narrower head. Mark is giving us both masterful head, sliding his mouth up and down our cranks, while twisting his head from side to side in long, skillful strokes. The kid's amazing! Is this something they teach in college? Makes me regret dropping out of high school.

I pull Mark to his feet and kiss him, my hands exploring his torso, pinching his nipples, playing with his ass. I lift his right arm and tongue his pit, savoring the sweet/bitter taste of man sweat. It's a taste I could get drunk on. My tongue crosses over to his left nipple and swirls around it. I nip it gently and feel Mark's body tremble under my hands. I do the same with his right nipple. My tongue slides down the smooth, hard ridges of his belly, past his stiff dick, and washes over those meaty balls of his. I take them both in my mouth and suck hard. Mark heaves a sigh just a hair's breadth shy of a groan. While I'm holding the kid's dickmeat in my hand, my tongue runs the length of his shaft. When I get to its red, engorged head, I plunge down and swallow it all, my beard pressing tight against his balls. Mark cries out, and I dive into a frenzy of cocksucking. The kid is good at giving head, but nobody eats dick as good as I do, and

I aim to prove it. I have the honor of the blue-collar working class to uphold.

Eddy reaches into a table drawer, pulls out a condom and slips it on. He wraps his powerful arms around Mark from behind and slowly impales his ass. Mark grimaces and Eddy pauses a bit before he continues working his dick in. It don't take long before he's plowing Mark's sweet young ass hard, driving his dickmeat home with ball-slammin' force.

My mouth glides up and down the shaft of the kid's dickmeat, my head twisting from side to side to increase the sensation for him. Between the two of us, the kid is getting worked over good. I can see he's well on his way to losing it big time. Mark's groans are bouncing off the rafters now, and his body is trembling like a leaf in a gale-force wind. He twists his head around and shoots Eddy a wild-eyed look, sweat streaming down his face. Eddy plants his mouth over Mark's and tongues him for all he's worth, at the same time reaching down and twisting the kid's nipples hard. Mark bucks between us like a bronco in heat, but we hold on, Eddy slamming hard into his ass, me feeding on his dick. I come up for air, sliding my spit-and-precum-slicked hand up and down Mark's crank. I feel his balls in my hand tighten up, and I know he's about ready to shoot.

A couple more strokes and he's over the edge. Mark yells loud enough to bring the roof down, and a mighty load of jism squirts out of his dickhead, splattering against my face and chest. Eddy roars soon after as he squirts his load into the condom up Mark's ass, his arms wrapped tight enough around the kid to damn near squeeze the air out of him. It just takes a few more strokes of my fist around my dick before I'm blasting my load halfway across the room as well. The two of them sink down beside me, and we kiss, Mark and Eddy licking the jism off my face. We collapse together in a heap on the rug by the fire and stay like that until the sky through the window starts turning light.

We drop the kid off at his car the next morning. "Take good care of those pictures," I tell him. "Not all of us agree with what's happening."

Mark and Eddy hug, and then Mark climbs into his car. I stick my head in the window and kiss him hard, my tongue slipping into his mouth. "Come back here some time soon," I growl, "or I'll have to head south and hunt you down."

Mark grins. "Wild horses couldn't keep me away," he says. He pulls away, Eddy and me just standing there, watching, as his car disappears into the distance.

"Some fun, eh?" Eddy says, winking at me.

I look at him and grin. "Hell, yeah, Eddy!" We laugh and climb back into the truck.

SWITCHBACK

Jonathan Asche

The cabin's rear window offered a glorious view of the lake, the fir trees marching up the foothills and, rising above it all, Switchback Mountain. But we hadn't come there for the view.

We sat on a big, L-shaped sectional; Tim and I between our hosts, Rick and Dennis. Condoms and lube sat on the coffee table. On the flat screen in front of us, a brawny guy was on his back gulping down a fat, uncut cock while a tattooed muscle hunk ate his furry ass. "It'll set the mood," Rick said when he put the disk into the DVD player.

Instead it increased the tension.

I looked over at Tim, sitting on my right, and got a weak smile. To the right of him was Rick, his angular face shaded by a sexy five o'clock shadow, sipping a Cape Cod, his eyes sliding our way to see if the action in the room had caught up with the antics on the screen. Sitting to my left was Dennis, his muscle-girded, fur-covered torso already bare. I'd admired Dennis's physique many times before, secretly and from afar. Now that I was free to ogle him without shame I found it difficult to look at him.

Dennis was casually rubbing the growing bulge in his shorts. When I caught his eye he leered.

On the TV screen one of the performers was now desperately sucking his two costars. For all the porn stars' efforts more blood was rushing to my face than to my dick.

I felt a hand on my thigh and instinctively looked at Tim, but I knew better: the hand was on my left leg. Instead of looking at Dennis my eyes stayed on Tim. He was rigid as a statue as Rick slowly stroked the back of his neck. The tent in Tim's plaid shorts revealed his rigidity extended below the waist. I got a flash memory of when Tim and I were first dating, ten years ago: Tim taking me to his claustrophobic studio apartment after a mutual friend's party. I remembered Tim casually stroking the back of my neck as we sat on his sofa talking, his touch having the same physical effect as Rick's was having on him now.

I had sworn I wouldn't get jealous, so I pretended I wasn't, quickly turning to Dennis. "Relax," he said, his hand easily sliding into my crotch, giving me a squeeze. His hands slipped lower, below my balls, until I felt his fingers pressing into my ass, making my asshole pulse.

Dennis leaned close enough for me to feel his warm breath against my ear. "I got somethin' for you," he drawled, his voice a velvet-on-gravel purr. He took my hand and placed it on the bulging fly of his olive-green cargo shorts. His cock throbbed beneath. Dark green wet spots made by his weeping dick made it plain he wore no underwear. "Go ahead and take it out," he encouraged.

I wanted to look at Tim, see if he was watching, see what he was up to, but I kept my eyes on my trembling hands as I gracelessly unzipped Dennis's shorts and rooted around inside.

A moment later, Dennis's cock—hard, thick, *big*—was out of his shorts and in my hand.

My face burned. A different kind of heat burned between my legs.

Dennis let out a deep, guttural groan. The bristly hairs of his beard tickled my nape and he muttered something unintelligible but unmistakably filthy. Soft moans came from the other side of the sofa, cutting through the forced grunts and obscene commands from the porno DVD. I wanted to turn my head, but...

Dennis's cock was *in my hand.*

I hadn't touched another man's cock since Tim and I got together. It took a few dates before I got my hands on his. Much as I wanted him at first meeting, we vowed to take it slow. "Slow" meaning precisely three dates, until that fateful night in his apartment, after that party, when he stroked my neck with one hand and my thigh with the other. We kissed, and then we couldn't get naked fast enough. I'd slipped my hand into Tim's underwear, wanting to feel his cock before I saw it. But Tim was impatient and pulled his briefs down, unveiling his veined hard-on. I was just as impatient to get it in my mouth.

Dennis looked at me expectantly, waiting for me to put my lips around his dick. I wanted to—my cock was aching for me to—but I couldn't bring myself to do more than gently stroke it.

I stood up. "I think it's time to get out of these clothes."

"Good idea," Dennis agreed, unbuttoning his shorts.

I peeled off my T-shirt, turning away before Dennis's shorts hit the floor, turning to see, finally, what Tim and Rick were up to. Things had progressed exponentially on their side of the sofa. Tim was nude, leaning back against the cushions, his eyes half-closed, with a beatific smile on his face. Rick, still wearing his shorts but with his cock out, knelt between Tim's spread thighs, swallowing his stiff dick in rhythmic gulps—the dick I had been sucking for the past ten years.

Tim noticed me, and his smile became a grin, as if to say, "Isn't this fun?" I wasn't sure if it was. I returned the grin, even as I felt a hot knife pierce my heart. I moved in quickly, kneeling on the sofa, leaning down and kissing Tim, hard and deep, pinching one of his nipples with equal brutality, relishing his sudden cry. Just a reminder: *he was mine.*

Then I was looking in Rick's face. He was grinning, his lips wet. Foamy globs of spit clung to his chin. Hands grabbed at the front of my shorts, unbuttoning them. Rick moved in to kiss me. It was a surprisingly tender kiss, his tongue slipping between my lips gently, as if testing the waters. I could taste the tart sweetness of the Cape Cod he drank earlier, and, I believed, Tim's cock. His tongue pushed deeper, and I instinctively responded in kind. Pleasure surged through me, humming through my stiff dick. Tim, sitting beneath us, was forgotten.

My shorts were pulled down with a quick tug and I was exposed. Dennis covered me just as quickly, his body heavy and warm across my back. His cock pressed into the smooth divide of my buttcheeks.

"You've got a *fine* ass," he hissed, grinding his hard-on against my ass. "You tell me, Tim, does Jamie's ass taste as sweet as it looks?"

I jerked away from Rick's soft lips, my eyes seizing on my lover's. Tim looked like he'd just been slapped across the face, and it made me perversely happy.

"Aren't you going to answer?" I teased, closing a hand around Tim's cock and stroking it idly.

Tim loved to eat ass—loved to eat *my* ass. I thought of all the marathon rim jobs he'd given me over the years, particularly remembering those indulgent moments when Tim would bury his face in my ass, licking, spearing and gnawing, making me thrash around the bed until I came. "I could eat your ass all day long," Tim would say, his voice thick with satisfaction, his face moist with sweat and spit. I'd respond: "And I could suck your dick all day." But by then Tim was so horny from tonguing my hole he usually got off a minute after I took his cock into my mouth. I didn't care: I happily drank his load just the same.

The memories had my prick pumping out thick drops of precum.

"Looks like he's about to find out," Tim replied haltingly.

Dennis's mouth moved down my back, leaving a trail of wet kisses along my spine. I kept my eyes on Tim's face and my hand on his cock, giving him an encouraging smile. "You're so hot," I whispered, cupping his balls, manipulating the heavy spheres in their hairy sac. I lowered my face toward his crotch...

A shiver of erotic pleasure stopped me before I reached my lover's cock. The tip of Dennis's tongue was circling my hole, making my asslips contract. I closed my eyes. "Oh, yes," I whimpered.

And then Dennis drove his tongue into my chute and I wailed. He pushed his face between my buttcheeks, feasting like a pig at a trough. His beard rubbed against my splayed ass like sandpaper as his tongue burrowed deep into my hole, making me weak.

Fingers beneath my chin tilted my face upward until I was eye level with a cock: Rick's cock. It wasn't as long as his lover's, but it was uncut, the thick foreskin rolled back revealing a fat, red, egg-sized head. I'd never been with a guy who had an uncut dick; Tim, five years older and ten times more experienced when we met, had. "He was Latino," Tim offered, as if an explanation was necessary. I had asked if he preferred his cocks uncut and he said he just liked cock, period. Then he went on about the fun he had with his uncut Latino ("a one-night stand that went on for three nights"), telling me about how he used to chew on his foreskin and push his tongue under that fleshy hood. The explicit detail was meant to turn me on, but all Tim aroused was envy. I was also mildly resentful: not only had he experienced something I hadn't, but the boundaries of our relationship precluded me from ever experiencing it in the future.

Until now.

"He's never had an uncut cock before," Tim said. His voice was flat and emotionless, but took on an edge when he added: "So I guess now we're even."

I looked up, finding Rick's smile at the top of his torso's tautly muscled horizon. He pushed his sticky cockhead against my lips. I returned the smile and then opened wide, taking his dick into my mouth, savoring his deep, satisfied moan almost as much as I savored his prick. As I sucked I continued to stroke Tim, though listlessly, without much thought. Rick's cock was the focus of my attention now, and I planned to enjoy every inch. I prodded the extra flesh beneath the corona. It was thick and plush and I couldn't resist nibbling on it.

Dennis plunged his tongue into my hole with such brutal force that I nearly lost my balance. Rick's cock muffled my cries, so the performers in the porno DVD, with their overacted groans, served as my proxy.

Then Rick pulled his dick from my mouth, leaving me gasping. He pushed his foreskin forward until it covered half his cockhead. A silvery trickle of precum oozed out his piss slit and I stuck out my tongue, catching his juice as it dripped off his dick. He let out a throaty chuckle as I tried to work my tongue beneath that sleeve of skin. There wasn't much, his hard-on taking up most of the slack. I wished I'd gotten to play with his cock when it was soft, really experiencing the novelty of that intriguing bit of skin—a natural penis accessory. As much fun as it was to play with a hard dick, I enjoyed getting a guy hard just as much. I'd often descend on Tim as he was getting out of the shower, getting ready for work. He'd protest—"You'll make me late!"—but he never pushed me away as I fondled his dangling prick. With the head resting on my tongue, I'd tease it with gentle flicks. I'd sink my face into his crotch, nuzzling his silky pubes, getting a whiff of his manly scent beneath the floral smell of soap. I'd suck on his balls, hanging low in their velvety sac. By the time I returned to his cock Tim already had a semi. Then I took it into my mouth, thrilled as I felt it swell between my lips.

Tim's cock slipping out of my hand reminded me of my lover's presence. I cut my eyes guiltily toward him, but the spot where he'd been sitting beneath us, Rick's cock and my head forming an arch over his lap, was vacant. He was now standing behind Rick, fingers digging into our cohost's asscrack. "I've always thought about eating this ass," Tim said.

The words stung. Dennis pulled me away, onto his lap, before they could do further damage.

My jealousy was disingenuous. I'd also always thought about eating Rick's ass, among other things. I'd thought about Dennis, too. Our mutual attraction to the couple was part of the reason why, after ten years of monogamy, proudly proving wrong our skeptical friends who cattily said we'd be renegotiating the terms of our commitment within five years—an inevitability in their roving eyes—we decided to risk our relationship for the sake of sexual variety. But Rick and Dennis's hotness wasn't the only reason Tim and I agreed to join them in Switchback Mountain.

Dennis wore a big grin. His beard was damp, his eyes wild. "I could eat that ass all day long," he said, seizing me, appropriately enough, in a tight, sweaty bear hug. The words sounded wrong coming from him. Those were Tim's words.

He kissed me, and I responded, just as I had when Rick kissed me. But suddenly kissing Dennis seemed wrong, too, an intimacy to be avoided. Silly, to draw the line at a kiss while letting him shove his tongue up my chute was perfectly fine. Well, this was supposed to be *just* sex. Kisses suggested more than that. But then I thought of Tim's admission to Rick about always thinking about eating his ass, and I returned Dennis's kiss with twice the passion. It was a wet, sloppy, *nasty* kiss.

Dennis's hand moved between my thighs, gripping my shaft and stroking it lightly. Precum flowed freely, coating Dennis's fingers. He put those fingers between his lips and sucked, whispering, "Sweet." He kissed me again while his hand returned to my cock to collect more juice. Then he brought his gooey fingers to my mouth, slipping them between my lips and commanding me to taste myself.

I closed my eyes. Our real orgy and the by-now-forgotten porno DVD filled the cabin with an X-rated din of slurps and smacks, grunts and groans, whispers and exclamations. In my mind I remembered hearing Tim, three months ago, telling me upon coming home from the gym: *"I almost cheated on you tonight."* I wasn't given a chance to absorb the shock of his admission before he launched into detail, telling me about the guy in the showers, playing with himself in the other stall, not caring that Tim was watching—*wanting* him to watch. Tim got so aroused he began jacking off too. The man stepped over into Tim's stall, and that's when Tim realized things had gone too far. "I grabbed my towel and ran into the steam room to"—his voice became meek—"regain my composure."

"At least you did that much," I said acidly. I said some other things as well, before I walked out the door.

But I came back two days later. And now...

"Oh, *yes!*" I cried.

Dennis hooked his index and middle fingers into my chute, pushing deep into me until he hit my prostate. "Just wait till I get my cock in there," he growled.

I wasn't sure I could. Every time his fingers sank into my warm hole my cock jumped and my body trembled. Distraction came from a loud moan piercing the air: I wondered who made it, Tim or Rick or the porn stars, and what had prompted it. I wanted to turn around and see, but then Dennis plunged his fingers into me and suddenly it was my moans filling the air.

"Come to see what the commotion was about?" Dennis chuckled.

Tim and Rick had come over to join us. Rick, smiling impishly, immediately knelt on the floor, placing one hand on my thigh, the other playing with his lover's balls. Tim remained standing, his glistening hard-on aimed at Dennis's head.

Dennis continued fingering my hole as he said to Tim: "This is one hot-assed boy you got here." The crude compliment was oddly thrilling.

Tim, wearing a dazed, distant look, nodded, his eyes going from my crotch to Dennis's while he stroked his dick, wondering how to proceed. Lucky for him, Dennis acted fast. He reached for Tim's dong, curling his fist around it. "You're pretty hot yourself," Dennis said, pumping Tim's cock.

I wondered if that's what the man at the gym said to Tim, when he joined him in the shower. Or did Tim speak first? As much as we talked about the incident, we never examined the details, just the ramifications. Hot, angry make-up sex had followed. I rode Tim like a crazed beast, squeezing my ass around his cock like I intended to pinch it off. After I came on his chest, I pissed all over him, delighting in his sputtering revulsion. Then I slept on the couch.

Dennis leaned forward and took Tim's boner between his

lips, sucking it gently. He pulled his mouth away, a thin string of spit hung suspended between Dennis's lower lip and the tip of Tim's cock, broken when Dennis smiled. Tim still wore that dazed, distant expression.

I shuddered. Rick was licking my cockhead, each swipe of his tongue bringing me closer to blowing my load. I pushed him away.

"Ease up, 'less you want a mouthful of cum," I said. Rick said: "Yum!"

But before I could flood Rick's mouth Dennis seized my arm and pushed me forward, off the sofa, urging me to get on the floor with his lover; urging me to suck his dick. I was pretty sure Dennis would be erupting in my mouth: his cock was now deep red and throbbing, with precum streaming down the shaft, collecting in the tangled hairs of his ball sac. It looked like it could blow at any second.

I touched my tongue to his pole, following the slick trail of nectar up to its source, slurping it down my throat loudly. A low groan rumbled in Dennis's throat like distant thunder.

"Oh, yes," he gurgled, running his fingers through my hair as I swallowed his dick. "Suck Daddy's cock. Get it ready for fucking that sweet ass of yours."

I kept sucking, drooling all over his stiff prick, so copiously that rivulets of saliva escaped my lips, soaking his balls and the sofa cushion.

"That's right," Dennis continued. "Daddy's boy knows how to treat a cock."

A hand seized my arm, pulling me away. Dennis's cock popped from my lips violently, slapping against his belly with a loud *thwack*. "Hey!" Dennis said, annoyed.

Once on my feet I found myself looking into Tim's eyes, filled with apologies, eagerness, desire—*love*.

It was a week after Tim admitted his temptation at the gym that we began to reconsider our monogamy. We were still in love, but our sex life had become routine. Would Tim be able to resist future temptations? Would I? "If we're going to see other people, I'd rather do it together," I said. Our plan was to have a threeway, but we knew Dennis and Tim had an open relationship—they were among the friends who thought long-term monogamy was impossible, that gay men who imposed such restrictions on themselves were delusional—and, of course, they were fucking hot. We settled on a foursome instead.

"You're not his daddy," Tim said. "His ass is *mine*." He was speaking to Dennis but his eyes were on me.

"C'mon, now," Dennis protested. "It's supposed to be share and share alike."

Sticky warm kisses landed on the base of my spine; hands caressed my butt. Rick, getting his licks in while he had the chance.

I didn't want Rick, and I didn't want Dennis. At that moment Tim and I realized what we wanted most of all:

"I want you to fuck me," I whispered.

Tim smiled and pulled my body against his, wrapping me in his arms, holding me tight. Our anguished cocks rubbed together, burning between us. Our mouths melded in a needy, violent kiss. I heard Dennis's voice but not what he said. It didn't matter.

Tim led me over to the far end of the sectional, snagging a bottle of lubricant off the coffee table on the way. We lubed up quickly, and within minutes I was lowering myself onto Tim's lap. Dennis had primed my ass well: Tim's cock slid in with relative ease, though with just enough tension to feel good. Tim's dick went into my hole like a hand into a glove.

Like we were made for each other.

A gasping groan later and his dick was all the way inside me, to the hilt. Tim was wearing the same beatific smile he wore earlier, when Rick was giving him a blow job. But there was something more in his eyes now, something that I knew was only for me. I wanted to say, "I love you, too." I didn't, though. I rolled my hips instead, squeezing my ass-muscles around his stiff cock, not violently like before but gently; I wanted to massage it, not snap it off.

Tim moaned loudly, thrusting into me. He gripped my asscheeks, digging into the firm flesh as he slammed his cock inside me. I held on to his shoulders, a cowboy holding on to a bucking bronco. I took one of Tim's hands away from my ass and brought it to my mouth, taking the fingers into my mouth and sucking them like I was sucking a cock. When Tim pulled his fingers from my mouth they were dripping wet with my spit. He wrapped those wet fingers around my dick, also dripping.

He stroked me, slowly, chuckling as I writhed on his lap. His thumb rubbed over my piss slit, and then he put it in his mouth, sucking off my juices. I swooped in to give him another taste of me, kissing him so hard I wondered if I might draw blood. We kept kissing and we kept fucking, Tim thrusting and me rolling.

Tim's hand returned to my cock, pressing it down onto his belly (still flat at thirty-eight). I began to undulate against his body, trembling from the hot friction created between his hand and his belly, both lubricated by my precum. Any second, Tim's belly was going to be covered in more viscous juices.

Our mouths separated. We looked each other in the eyes. Tim whispered, so soft only I could hear: "I love you so much." That's when I came.

Tim marveled at my copious load splattering his chest and abs. "Feed it to me," he commanded.

I raked my fingers through a creamy puddle of cum that had collected on his sternum and brought them to his mouth. He sucked the jizz off my fingers hungrily. My cock throbbed at the sight.

"Now it's your turn," I said, rolling my hips.

He seized me in his arms and rocked forward, hammering my ass in quick, sharp strokes. A wracking sob announced his orgasm.

"Yes, baby, yes," I sighed as his cock exploded inside me.

Other cries filled the room. I looked over my shoulder in time to see Dennis in the final spasms of coming while Rick, sitting next to him, stroked his dick. Dennis pulled Rick to him, kissed him, then pushed Rick's face toward his crotch to lap up his load.

"Eat that ass!" barked one of the performers in the porno movie, sounding more absurd than sexy. I couldn't help but giggle.

"You guys were *hot*," Dennis said, shaking his head like he couldn't believe it.

I looked at Dennis, sprawled on the sofa, his burly body covered in a sheen of sweat; at Rick, curled beside him, happily licking his lover's cock. They were hot, too, and I looked at them because I knew this was the last time I'd see them this way.

I replied to Dennis's compliment with a smile then I turned away.

"Yes," I said to Tim, my hands caressing his chest, "we *are* hot."

TOKENS

Pepper Espinoza

J ake draped his long frame over the bed with a cigarette dangling between his teeth, tousled and bathed in easy confidence. He was out of step with time, being born fifty years too late to wear a fedora and spats convincingly. He could have been French, or maybe Italian; something Mediterranean and sun kissed, his dark blue eyes heavy with sleep, or desire, or a secret joke he had no intention of sharing. He was always in danger of looking smug, but that tendency was offset by his gregariousness, and instead of being annoyed by the smirk playing on the corners of his lips, Ian found himself charmed.

"You have time for a smoke, don't you?" Jake asked, holding his cigarette out, the lit tip pointed at himself.

Ian didn't have time for a smoke, but that didn't stop him from taking it and closing his lips around the slightly damp butt. He puffed at the filter, his eyes locked on Jake's upturned face while the smoke swirled around his head. This was a nonsmoking room, and Jake knew it, but his credit card wasn't on file. Oh, well, the damage was already done, and the nicotine did wonders for his nerves. But the small progress was lost when Jake's smirk shifted into a sincere smile, and he pulled a second smoke from the pack on the night table.

"Why are you in such a hurry anyway? Hot date tonight?"

"No. Why would you think that?"

Jake shrugged one lazy shoulder. "It's Valentine's Day. Shouldn't you be seen at the finest restaurant with a beautiful woman?"

"Is it? I guess I didn't notice."

"Well, that explains the lack of flowers."

Ian couldn't tell if Jake's disappointment was genuine or a mere tease, so he set about searching for his shoes, trailing ash and smoke behind him as he stalked across the room. Every time he met Jake, he promised himself he'd kick his shoes off right at the door, so they'd be available at the earliest possible convenience. It was difficult to flee barefoot, and if he didn't get out while Jake still basked in the after-glow, his plans for the entire afternoon—and sometimes the evening too—would be fucked. Perhaps Jake knew all this and made it a point to hide Ian's shoes while Ian was otherwise distracted. Knowing Jake the way he did, Ian wouldn't put it past him.

"Did you even try to find a date?" Jake asked.

"No. I really don't pay attention to greeting card holidays."

"Greeting card holidays?"

"Yeah, you know, the holidays created by Hallmark so we can all feel a little extra guilty if we don't shell out hard-earned money on worthless trinkets."

"Ah. You're one of those."

"One of those what?"

"One of those people who thinks you figured out some great

truth about holidays, like the rest of us don't know how utterly meaningless it all is."

"If everybody's aware of how meaningless it all is, why do people celebrate it?"

"I don't know, Ian." Jake's lighter flickered to life and his cigarette glowed cherry red. "For fun? Because it's a convenient excuse and time to let people know we care? Because free chocolate is always great? Take your pick."

"Well, if those are the reasons to celebrate Valentine's Day, then you can still count me out."

"You're a romantic at heart."

Ian made a sound of triumph as he spotted his left shoe in the back of the closet. How it had managed to get past the closed door and wedge itself between the luggage rack and the wall, Ian didn't know, though he had his suspicions. But that just introduced a new mystery—how could Jake take the time to hide his shoes when he'd spent most of the past hour on his knees?

"I haven't got one."

"A heart? Yes, you have. It's just buried under layers of indifference."

"And there it will stay. Help me out here, will you?"

"No."

Ian sighed and pulled his shoe on. "Not all of us have the time to laze around hotels, okay?"

"Have dinner with me tonight, and I'll give you your shoe."

"Don't you have plans? I figured you'd have two or three dates lined up for tonight."

"I like to keep my options open."

"I don't know, Jake."

"What's there to know? You need to eat just like everybody else, and I'm offering to buy you dinner."

"I don't need anybody to buy me dinner. I'm perfectly capable of buying my own meals."

"That's not the point."

Ian stepped into the bathroom, surveyed the area to make sure his other shoe hadn't wandered in there by mistake, and flicked his cigarette stub into the toilet. "I know it's not. Seriously, though." He emerged again, his wayward gaze drifting back to Jake's perfect body. It would be much easier to find his shoe if Jake wasn't so damned distracting. Ian was sure of it. How could he concentrate on anything as mundane as footwear when Jake stretched his supple body in the sunshine and rubbed his fingers along his stomach in a thoughtless, sated way? "Don't you have plans?"

"You know my plans are flexible. Isn't that what you like about me?"

It was a major selling point, though by no means the sole basis of Ian's attraction to the other man. It was true that he liked having the number of somebody who could drop everything at a moment's notice when Ian called. Jake didn't play games with him, didn't hem and haw around the issue, didn't make Ian wait. He wasn't even sure what Jake did that allowed him so much flexibility, but the hours were great, and judging by the way Jake dressed, the money wasn't anything to sneeze at.

"Well, my plans aren't."

"You just said you didn't have any."

"I don't. Not of the romantic variety. I still have work to do."

"It won't go anywhere if you take the night off."

"Look, Jake, I appreciate the invitation. I really do. But I'm just not the romantic Valentine type. Now if you could just help me..."

Jake produced the missing shoe from behind a pillow. "If

you want your shoe, you're going to have to come and get it."

"Hang on. How did my shoe end up behind your pillow?"

Jake shrugged. "This isn't even the strangest place to find it. You're a maniac if you haven't had it in a while."

"I'm not a maniac."

"You're a bit maniacal." He waved the shoe at Ian and wagged his eyebrows. "I was serious about you coming to get it."

"It's a trap."

"Possibly. I am the suspicious type. My own mother thinks I've got shifty eyes."

"I really do have to go."

"That may be, but you're not going anywhere without this shoe."

"Put your cigarette out."

"Ooh. Sounds like I'm in for a bit of the rough stuff," Jake said, but he obediently snubbed the cigarette out in an empty glass. He brought the shoe up to his nose and inhaled, his attention never leaving Ian's face. With his gaze locked, he pushed his pink tongue between his bruised lips and delicately licked over the top of the shoe, letting his tongue linger on the leather in the most obscene way. Ian's groin tightened, his cock starting to rise like he hadn't just fully sated himself on Jake's all-too-willing flesh.

Ian dived onto the bed, arm outstretched to snag the shoe, but Jake was too quick. He hid it behind his back, out of reach, his blue eyes dancing with pleasure at the minor mischief. Ian outweighed him by twenty or so pounds, and he probably could have tossed Jake out of the way easily enough, but he ended up tackling the younger man instead, which led to Jake sneaking his arms around Ian, catching him in a steel grip. Ian should have been annoyed by the very obvious and not at all subtle ploy, but that wouldn't exactly be fair to Jake. After all, it had been quite obvious and about as subtle as a hammer to the kneecap. It was Ian's own fault for getting himself trapped in that position.

Jake shifted beneath him, rolling his hips upward, proving beyond a shadow of a doubt that he was not yet sated by the afternoon's activities. Ian groaned, his cock responding to the rigid length pressed resolutely against his thigh. The taste of cigarettes and tropical punch gum greeted Ian as he pushed his tongue past Jake's lips, and the familiar combination of flavor did more to make him light-headed than the expert way Jake moved his mouth. Nobody had ever tasted like Jake, and since the night they met, that heady joining of the sweet and musky only signaled one thing—that Ian was in for one hell of a ride.

The kiss was almost identical to the thousands they shared before it. They had the tendency to start out slow, determined to take their time, but impatience always got the better of them. Ian buried his fingers in Jake's dark hair, clutching at him while he shoved his tongue back between Jake's welcoming lips. He did have errands and work waiting for him—that hadn't been bullshit—but Jake's fingers dancing over his spine were extremely convincing. They moved up and down his back, warm and gentle through his silk shirt, full of sleepy promises. His cock pressed painfully against his zipper, ready to burst through his fly.

"Please," Jake moaned, his other hand sliding between their bodies.

"Please? Please what?"

"Please fuck me."

"I already fucked you once today. Isn't that enough?"

"No," Jake answered promptly. He took Ian's hand and guided it to his throbbing shaft. Ian sighed and fisted his length, pumping it once because he loved the smooth skin and the implacable hardness. "When it comes to you, there's no such thing as enough."

Ian caught Jake's mouth in another hard kiss, which was far preferable to meeting Jake's bright gaze. He had sharp eyes, and sooner or later, he would see just how much it affected Ian when he talked like that. Or maybe he had already seen? Perhaps that was why he took such pleasure in reminding Ian how much he wanted him. But he'd always been a very, very blunt young man, so his eagerness now wasn't anything extraordinary.

"Fuck me," Jake panted into Ian's mouth. "Take me."

"Aren't you a bit tender?" Ian asked with unusual delicacy.

"I like it better when I'm a bit tender. It's best when I'm a bit tender and you're pounding into me like you want to break me."

"I don't have—"

"Time? Then stop talking and start doing."

"I was going to say a condom."

"Oh, there's one on the nightstand."

Ian pushed himself to his knees, tugging at his zipper with a groan of relief. Yes, he did have schedules. No, he didn't have the time for this. But Jake was stretched out beneath him like a sumptuous banquet, every inch of his body a divine treat, and Ian loved nothing more than indulging himself on the smooth skin and finely carved muscles and sensitive flesh. Jake snagged the condom and tore the foil, nudging it over Ian's thick head as soon as he had the zipper down.

Ian slipped his fingers between Jake's thighs, the tips of his middle and index fingers sliding over Jake's slick and stretched opening. Jake hissed at the first brush of contact, arching off the bed and into the caress. The heat from his skin was unbelievable, teasing Ian with the promise of more before he pushed his fingers into the tight passage. Jake moaned and began to rock, fucking himself on Jake's fingers without missing a beat. Jake was happy just to watch him for a long moment, noting the way his muscles shifted beneath his skin each time he flexed around the intrusive digits. He really was an amazing specimen, a work of art.

His admiration for Jake's body went beyond lust or love. One didn't fall in lust or in love with a work of art. He couldn't say he wanted to fuck Michelangelo's *David* or take the *Mona Lisa* up the ass—though the respective artists might have been game for a ride or two. If he'd been an artist himself, he would have made Jake his muse. But he wasn't an artist, and when he existed in his normal life and his regular world, some would call him downright soulless. His feelings on holidays were just one piece of evidence among many for that particular assertion.

"I'm ready," Jake said, face twisting into what could have as easily been pain as desire. "God, Ian, I'm ready."

"You're always ready," Ian muttered, guiding his cock to Jake's waiting hole.

Jake caught Ian by the back of the neck and pulled him into a close embrace. "I'm not the slut you think I am," he said, breath and words hot against Ian's ear. "You're the only one."

Before Ian could consider the implications in that statement, Jake was moving against him, lifting his hips to meet Ian's rigid cock. He pushed down, forcing the length inside of him, his walls clamping down like a vise around him. At first, they were both silent except for ragged gasps and aborted moans that meant *more*, but Jake was soon swept up in the pleasure and his defenses crumbled. Ian only understood one garbled word in ten, the French falling from Jake's mouth fluid to the point of incomprehensibility, like water breaking over rounded boulders and gurgling streams merging into great rivers.

Ian always secretly loved the way Jake babbled when his control started to slip. It wasn't always French. Sometimes it was Spanish, sometimes Italian, and sometimes it was the harder guttural stops of German. Ian never asked, but he often speculated on just where Jake had come from. An army brat seemed the most elegant explanation. It was hard to imagine the flighty, sweet-spirited Jake being the son of some hard-nosed Army general, but strangely appropriate, too. He fucked like he'd seen the world and picked up a few tricks along the way.

"Harder," Jake begged, fingernails digging into Ian's spine. The stinging crescents spurred Ian to comply, though it occurred to him that he was just a little too old for this sort of thing. Not too old for Jake in particular—a ten-year age difference was nothing when he was this close to forty—but too old to have sex three times in an afternoon, too old to obey every plea and whimper until his heart was beating so hard against his ribs he thought it was in danger of exploding. But he did fuck Jake harder, and faster, until the sound of damp skin slapping against skin echoed louder than their harsh breathing.

When they'd first started fucking, Ian tried to limit himself to one or two meetings a month. That seemed a reasonable limit, giving him something to look forward to without infringing too much on his regular life. That had been so important when he'd finally given in to the desire for Jake's body. There had been plenty of women in the twenty years since he reached sexual maturity, but Jake was the first man, and their couplings had felt so illicit, heady in their novelty. Jake was no longer what Ian would call a novelty, but only because their meetings were no longer what anybody would call rare. Ian craved the smell of Jake's skin, the exquisite shape of him, too much to be patient. A week? How could Ian survive a week without feeling Jake fold himself around his body and breathe broken pleas into his ears? Now it seemed like they were meeting every other day, their desire only fed by their time together, not slaked.

Jake moaned, the sound carrying just a hint of frustration. That was Ian's only warning before Jake clutched him with both arms and rolled him onto his back. Ian didn't protest as Jake rose above him, settling himself before slamming back. He arched back, the tendons in his neck and shoulders sharply defined against his pale skin. Ian reached up to caress each nipple, teasing and squeezing the hard flesh between his thumb and forefinger. Each time he pinched the puffy skin, Jake clenched around him, his tight walls bearing down hard on Ian's cock. His chest was a healthy shade of pink, gleaming with salty deliciousness. And every twinge, every shudder, every shiver and moan, every beautiful shade of pink and cream, was Ian's. Lifelong addictions were formed by experiences less divine than this.

The unmistakable shape of a shoe pressed against Ian's shoulder blade. He smiled and pulled Jake down into a slow kiss, his mouth moving in marked contrast to the rhythm of their hips. His cock slammed into Jake's ass, but his tongue barely teased the corner of his mouth, slowly exploring the soft curves, losing himself in the taste once again. Sometimes, when their hearts seemed to be beating in time, and they shared every breath, and Ian didn't give a second thought to his carefully planned schedule, he thought maybe there should be something more between them. Something like a romantic dinner and a bottle of fine wine.

Jake's teeth snagged Ian's lips, and between the coppery taste of blood and the earthier taste of salt, he moaned that he was so fucking close. "Please, oh, fuck, please."

Ian still had the wherewithal to reach for the sheet, wrapping the rich material around Jake's cock and pumping his wrist in a hard stroke. Jake went rigid, fluttering and grinding around Ian's shaft as hot come erupted from him. The wet cloth clung to his skin, and Ian stroked him until he was nearly sobbing, far too sensitive to withstand the abuse. Jake felt a little bad for that, but not enough to stop. Not when he clutched around Ian so tightly, and used his hips and thighs and quivered and cried out. Ian could only take advantage of this tight pleasure for a few seconds—that felt like years—before it was too much for him. His muscles spasmed, his cock jerking hard, filling the tip of the condom.

"Tell me the truth," Ian said, lips brushing over Jake's damp hair.

"About what?"

"Do you hide my shoes?"

"Not usually. But I know how to take advantage of good opportunities when I see them."

Ian caressed Jake's neck, tracing random patterns on his nape, where the short hair met his skin. Jake felt good, solid and settled and a perfect fit against Ian's frame.

"I'm not keeping you from something super important, am I?" Jake asked sleepily.

"Not super important, no."

"So you don't mind staying for a bit longer?"

"I can't," Ian said, closing his eyes against the disappointment he knew would be painting Jake's face. "That's the point of an afternoon quickie, isn't it?"

"You've been here since noon."

"Yeah. So?"

"It's three-thirty. We've already defeated the purpose of an afternoon quickie."

"That just means I have things to catch up on."

"Then have dinner with me tonight."

"We don't have dinner."

"True. But there's no law that says we *can't* have dinner. Come on, Ian, let's have a date. You might like it."

"You know, if we have a proper date, that means you can't attack me at the table or eat the dessert off me."

"I'm capable of exercising self-control," Jake claimed, his words muffled as he nuzzled against Ian's throat. "And we can get the dessert to go." His teeth scraped over Ian's Adam's apple. "This doesn't have to mean anything more than what it is. A friendly dinner."

"A friendly dinner on Valentine's Day? Is that even possible?"

"Sure. It can mean whatever we want it to mean."

Ian extricated himself from Jake's sticky hold, grabbing the shoe from the bed before he stood. A quick glance at him confirmed he couldn't go back to the office like this. Before, he would have been able to claim a long lunch with a client, where the whiskey and the stories were both flowing freely. But now his silk shirt was too rumpled, his trousers too wrinkled, and there was a mysterious and damning stain on his fly. By the time he returned home, showered, changed and drove back to work, it would be after five. He should have been annoyed, but how could he regret this time with Jake?

"We'd never get reservations at a decent place," Ian pointed out. "Everything's probably been booked for months."

Jake laughed. "I don't care where we eat. You could take me to McDonalds. This is just a friendly dinner, remember?"

Ian nodded, but he knew better. If he took Jake out anywhere, it would have to mean more than just two guys sharing a table and splitting the tab, if only because Jake *deserved* more.

"I'm not going to take you to McDonalds. I know the chef at Table 29. He might be able to get us a reservation."

"Are you serious?"

"Yes. Why? Don't you want to go to Table 29?"

"Who wouldn't want to eat there?"

"People who don't enjoy gastronomical experiments, I suppose."

Jake's smile was lopsided and pleased. Ian already had a pretty thorough mental catalogue of Jake's smiles, and he was undeniably pleased for having caused this one. "You're sure?"

"Yes. I'll even pick you up at your house like a proper date."

"You're like my very own Prince Charming."

"But if I'm going to take you out tonight, I've really got to be going now."

Jake nodded. "I'll text you my address. What time should I expect you?"

"Eight, unless Isabel can't get us a table."

"I'll be ready."

Ian straightened his clothes as best as he could, putting on his other shoe and securing his buckle. Jake was stretched out on the bed again, another unlit cigarette in his fingers, and a relaxed grin lighting his face. Maybe tonight would be the night Ian learned just where he came from and the answers to a thousand other mysteries he'd mulled over but could never bring himself to ask about. Maybe he'd even speak a bit of French or Italian for Ian's pleasure, his full lips gliding gracefully over the words, forming them perfectly between his tongue and teeth.

"I've never had a boyfriend," Ian blurted.

Jake winked. "I know."

"Doesn't that bother you?"

"It doesn't bother me if it doesn't bother you. I'm certainly not going to complain. You seem to know what you're doing, after all."

If he did, it was only because of his willingness to follow Jake's amazing example. "Then I'll see you tonight."

"Happy Valentine's Day."

Ian paused at the door, looking over his shoulder to steal one final glimpse. It didn't matter that he would see Jake again in a few hours, or that he had already spent hours staring at him. The cigarette jutted from his lips at a jaunty angle, and the late afternoon sun spilled through the window, drawing the golden highlights out in his hair and hinting at the freckles dotting his nose. Maybe he would stop on his way and buy Jake a box of chocolates. And a flower to wear in his buttonhole. The tokens couldn't even begin to express the fondness he felt welling up in his chest, but they might make a good start.

ONE
AFTERNOON IN
THE BIBLE BELT

Jeff Mann

D elays, delays. First, there's hard rain on I-81. Gray clouds
swirl over June-green Virginia hills; wind whips the trees.
It's a goddamn downpour, so violent that most drivers put on
their hazard blinkers and pull off the road to wait it out.

"Oh, fuck. Oh, for fuck's sake." Cussing is my customary
response to adversity; John, perpetually calm, keeps driving,
albeit slowly. Then there's a traffic backup on I-26 as we
approach Asheville: roadwork. Then another backup as we leave
Asheville: car accident. We're crawling, not speeding, south.

I cuss some more; I check my wristwatch; I tap the dash-
board restlessly. "You told him two, right? We're gonna be late.
You know I hate to be late."

John shrugs. "Nothing to be done about it, Jeff." After thir-
teen years together, he's as used to a Leo's hotheaded impatience
as I'm used to a Virgo's cool equanimity.

His iPhone chirps. "Song of the horny Cajun," John says,
smiling, as he checks the text message. "Yep, it's Mr. Trey. He

wants to know if he can bring wine. Tension-reducer, he says."

"Hell, sure. As long as he drinks most of it." I'm fifty; John is forty-six. We're both at the age where alcohol seriously interferes with sexual functioning. Today, as much as I enjoy a good buzz, I think I'll postpone drinking till after our tryst with Trey.

"Here," John says, handing me his iPhone. "Text him. Tell him to bring wine; tell him we're leaving Asheville now. We should get there in twenty minutes."

"You're so bossy," I growl. I try to type a message, make mistakes, cuss more. "I hate this goddamn thing. How do all the young people do it? These keys are too small for my fingers." Grumbling, I fumblingly compose; grumbling, I hit SEND.

Half an hour late, we pull into the parking lot. It's a Holiday Inn Express, a few miles outside Hendersonville, North Carolina. I've read about this town online. Full to the brim with straights, Republicans, and devout Christians. Ugh. Sounds like where I grew up: too many churches and children. It's delicious to think that we'll be enjoying ourselves in such an insufferably righteous region. I have enough of the bad boy left in me to relish this sense of getting away with something behind judgmental backs.

John grabs our travel bag, I heft my bulging black leather backpack over my shoulder, and we head into the Holiday Inn. During check-in, I lay on my habitual Southern charm: "Ma'am, that's a mighty pretty necklace. Is that a golden sand dollar? And those lobby flowers—what kind are they?—they're pretty too. Y'all sure keep this place neat." What does she think of us, I wonder—John with his neat, casual, blue and khaki clothes, his golden hair and Yankee aloofness, and me with my shaved head, graying bush of a goatee, brown cargo shorts, black-leather wristband, and black muscle-shirt displaying bulky arms and copious tattoos. Surely she assumes we're queer, since we're getting a king-size bed. If only she knew in what perverse manner we'll soon be entertaining a guest.

Room 240—John texts Trey the number. We've barely had time to kick off our shoes, brush our teeth and piss when there's a knock at the door. Ah, the eagerness of youth. I open it, and there he is, smiling shyly.

Sweet cub. He's adorable, dressed in a black T-shirt and gray camo shorts. The goatee's gone since we first met, a month ago during my annual visit to New Orleans—probably shaved off for this professional conference he's attending. Instead, his cheeks and jaw are covered with tasty black stubble I can't wait to lick. His eyes and eyebrows are dark; his hair's thick and black, with big sideburns. Something about him reminds me of a preacher's son looking to get into trouble. We hug. I savor the solidity, the stockiness of him: broad shoulders, small hips, sexy bit of belly.

"Glad this worked out," I say, leading him into the room. "I figured we wouldn't see you again till next May when we get back to N'Orleans."

"I'm glad too. Thanks for driving down here," Trey says. "I brought some Riesling." He pulls a blue bottle of Schmitt Söhne from a paper bag. "I'm kind of nervous, you know? Do you mind?"

"Go for it." His anxiety is endearing, but I don't tell him that. Instead, I fetch plastic cups from the bathroom and pour us all wine. John and I sip small amounts, leaving him the lion's share.

We catch up: our recent trip to DC Leather Pride, the details of Trey's conference here in Hendersonville. "Keith's totally fine with this," he assures us, stretching out on the bed. "He wants me to explore whatever turns me on."

"Let's hear it for permissive husbears," I say, winking at

John. Bless him, he insisted on monogamy for our first few years together, but, with him vanilla and me increasingly perverse, an open relationship is the only way we could have made it this far, and we both know it. He has his occasional Grindr tricks, and I have my BDSM fuckbuddies with whom I play infrequently. It's rare, though, that we get to share a cub as hot as Trey. And, Daddy Bear that I am, I *have* been looking for a part-time boy.

I may be oversexed and kinky, a guy who looks like he just stepped out of a redneck beer joint or big-city leather bar, but, truth is, I'm shy and insecure. John's the one who always gets things started. He's hungrier, maybe, or just more assertive and confident. Trey's only halfway through his wine before John sits on the bed's edge and starts kissing him. I sit back, grinning and sipping. It's sweet and hot to see my handsome husbear making out with this burly boy. I prop my bare feet up and let them go at it. When my wine's finished, I rise, unzip my heavy backpack and pull out neatly cinched hanks of camo rope. I stand at the foot of the bed, where, shirtless by now, John and Trey are stretched out side by side, necking furiously, golden and black body hair creating a beautiful contrast.

"Ready to be tied up? I brought everything you asked for."

Trey nods. "Oh, yeah!" He sits up, eyes glowing. John sits back, ready to watch the bondage master break in another one.

Trey's very happy. I can tell by the high flush in his face, the excitement in his long-lashed brown eyes. This is exactly what he came for.

He's naked except for a jockstrap, on his knees in the middle of the bed. The rope's knotted around his wrists, securing them behind his back. It cinches his upper arms to his sides, runs under his beefy tits, makes an X across his upper chest. I haven't tied a boy in a while, but, makeshift as it is, I must admit the bondage looks mighty nice against the thick black swirls and curls of his chest hair. It sure seems to please Trey; we all know he isn't going anywhere till I decide to free him. Naked save for my black-leather wristband, I stand before him on the bed, holding his head in my hands, stroking his wavy, sweat-moist hair. Enthusiastically, expertly, he sucks me.

He's so good that already I'm getting close. I pull out, slip off the bed, fetch another toy from my overfull backpack. "Time for this." It's a black Wiffle-ball gag I picked up at the Leather Rack in DC only last week. "Should make you drool real pretty."

Trey nods assent. Kneeling before him, I push the ball between his teeth, fumble with the buckle behind his head, and now he's silenced.

"Ummm," he grunts. "Mmm."

"You like this? Can you breathe all right?"

He nods, mustering a faint smile around the gag.

"Good to hear. Do you know how fucking hot you look?"

Trey shakes his head and rolls his eyes. I kiss him, licking the taut curves of his lips, the black perforated ball. "I told you in New Orleans the only way you could look any hotter is to be bound and gagged," I whisper, wrapping my arms around him and pressing my face to his. "And so here you are."

Carefully, I ease him onto his back, then rope his feet together. John and I take turns sucking his nipples: tasty little things, the right one pierced with a delicate ring I tug with my teeth. Trey moans against his gag and closes his eyes. "For your husband," says John, standing back to snap a few photos with the iPhone. I massage Trey's hard jock-bulge, run my fingers through his thick belly hair, wipe clear droplets of drool off his chin.

There are two things I can't stay away from once I have a bottom roped and gagged: nips and asshole. Having feasted on the former, it's time for the latter.

"On your belly," I say, nudging Trey. Obediently, awkwardly, he rolls over. His back's broad, tapered, lightly hairy. Rope runs in a tight horizontal across his shoulder blades, circling both biceps, securing his arms together. Crossed at the wrists and thickly roped, his bound hands lie helplessly in the patch of fur dusting the small of his back. His butt's beautiful. Pale, solid mounds sprinkled with hair, a thicker growth in the crevice between.

The boy needs opened up for what's next. I untie his ankles and part his thighs, kneeling between them. Spreading his cheeks, I kiss and nip each buttock, then lick his crack from top to bottom. Lapping at the cloud of fur around his hole, I spread his cheeks wider and tongue-burrow up inside him. He tastes as good as I knew he would, musky and clean. His hole's bittersweet, the tight center of a flesh-flower.

"You might need these." John joins us on the bed, ribbed blue dildo and tube of lube in hand.

"Yes, indeed." I moisten Trey's little opening, then slowly slide one lubed forefinger inside him. "Sweet, hot and tight. Good boy," I whisper. Groaning, Trey spreads his thighs wider, pushing back onto me. John, nestling beside me, probes a bit, then slowly slips his lubed forefinger in beside mine. We finger-fuck Trey together, moving in and out in tandem.

"I think he's ready for Ole Blue," I say. We pull out; I grease up the dildo. John helps Trey onto his back, hoisting our captive's legs in the air. Trey shudders and sighs as I slide the dildo home.

"Feel good?" I pull the blue dick all the way out, then push it into him again and start a regular pumping.

Trey nods vigorously. John bends to kiss him, to nuzzle his nipples.

"How are your hands?" I say. "All right?"

"Mmm-huh."

"Breathing still all right?"

Another nod.

Hot as the boy looks with a ball strapped in his mouth, he's still new to all this, and I don't want to overdo it. "Take over for me," I say, pulling the dildo out and handing it to John. While John continues Trey's fuck, I unbuckle the gag and pull the spit-wet Wiffle-ball out.

"Thanks," Trey gasps. "But if you all keep fucking me like that, I'm gonna cum."

"Oh, no you don't!" John laughs. Removing Ole Blue, he pads toward the bathroom to rinse off the toy. "We've just gotten started."

"Right!" I say, tousling the sweaty waves of dark hair on Trey's temples. "No coming for you just yet, cublet. You had enough of being roped up?" I lift Trey's cup of wine to his mouth and give him a few gulps.

"Oh, no. I'm fine. Please leave me tied."

"'Sir.' Say 'Sir.'" I pinch his pierced nipple.

Trey winces and grins. "Please leave me tied, *Sir*."

"Good boy. Right answer." He seems to savor being bound as much as I savor keeping him bound. I think of our meeting last month in that Bourbon Street pub and give a silent prayer of thanks to the gods of kink. I stretch out, push Trey's head onto my cock and ride his face; happily, he bobs and laps. John returns from the bathroom to take more iPhone pics.

"Time this boy got fucked," I announce. "You want fucked?" Trey nods around his slurping mouthful of dick. John gets out the condoms and we both lube up.

John's first, hoisting Trey's legs in the air. Our bottom-boy grunts with pain as the fat head of John's cock first eases into him, but soon enough he's gasping "Oh, yeah!" and locking his thighs around John's waist. John's narrow hips cock back, slam forward, cock back, slam forward with increasing speed. I've hardly had time to prop myself up on pillows to enjoy the show when my husbear shakes, bucks into Trey, then pulls out and skins off the latex. Face knotting up, he cums all over Trey's belly hair—one jet, then another, then another—and falls across him panting.

John rolls drowsily off. He stretches and chuckles. "Wow! That was superb." Absentmindedly I finger-paint with John's semen, smearing it over Trey's belly and chest. I rise on one elbow, pushing a clean finger up Trey's asshole. "Me next," I say. "You can take some more, right?"

"Oh, yes," Trey says, giving me a sheepish grin. "A lot more." In a few seconds, my cock's sheathed up, Trey's calves are propped on my shoulders, and I'm sliding slowly up his ass. I look down at his flushed face, look down at my hard flesh moving in and out of his young body. I bend down, kiss him hard, chew gently on his pierced nipple, then, jacking his cock, ride him faster, shove into him deeper.

"Damn, boy, you feel so good." I grit my teeth and close my eyes. "I've been wanting up your ass ever since I first saw you."

"Don't cum inside me," Trey says. "Please, Sir. I want to be safe. I promised Keith."

"No way, buddy. Don't worry." I pick up my pace, getting closer to the crest, damned glad I didn't drink much wine. Bible-Belt butt-fucking's a helluva lot more fun than an afternoon buzz. In another minute I'm following John's lead, pulling out only to peel off the condom and pour myself in pearly clumps onto Trey's already cum-sticky torso.

I drowse atop him for a minute or two before remembering another of Trey's emailed requests. Rising, I fetch more supplies from my backpack. "Chew on this for a while," I say, peeling

Trey's jock off his loins only to cram it in his mouth. John fetches a wet washcloth, I cover Trey's pubes with shaving cream, and—while Trey looks on, wide-eyed, teeth sunk in the ribbed fabric, giving an occasional rapt, jock-gagged groan—John carefully and methodically shaves our captive's scrotum.

"Nice, pink and smooth," I say, wiping the residue of foam off before taking his sac into my mouth and nibbling softly. John and I take turns, deep-throating him, chewing his balls, till he erupts, his cum joining our semen's sticky mess on his belly.

"I think you've probably had enough for now," I say, unknotting the rope binding Trey, freeing first his torso and arms and finally his wrists. The postcoitus cuddle is brief, however. Our horny Cajun is soon ready for more. For a moment, I fear that two old bears like us might not be able to keep up with this young guy, but it takes our skillful cub little time to suck us both into full erection. This time we spit-roast him, Trey rocking and moaning on his elbows and knees, John riding his ass while Trey chokes and slobbers on my cock. John's done in no time—a load on the furry small of Trey's back—and heads to the bathroom to wash up. I take my place behind Trey, grasp his hips, and eagerly shove into him. I've barely started pounding his butt when he tosses his head and pushes back onto me, driving me into him deeper still. Quivering, he gasps, bows his head and goes limp.

I stop thrusting. "Damn, boy, did you just cum?"

He looks back over one shoulder with another smile, a combination of embarrassed and mischievous. "Yeah. I just love getting plowed. Sorry I made a mess on your all's sheets."

Reluctantly I pull out. "So, my guess is you don't want to be fucked any more?"

"No. I'm really sorry. But...here." He turns, spits in his

palm, unpeels my condom and goes to town. His hand's a blur. About forty seconds later, I'm leaning against him panting, and he's cupping my second load in his hand.

No all-night snuggle, which is the postscript we've all hoped for. I want to keep Trey in between us all night, his hands tied before him and a bandana knotted between his teeth, with his butt ready for us to plunder again before morning. But his conference schedule is too packed, and so, with hugs all around, he departs. Who knows when we'll see him again? I want to send his husbear a thank-you card, just for being kind enough, man enough, to share such a submissive sweetheart.

It's a hot June evening. Downtown Hendersonville's a long strip of cute shops and restaurants, with a gold-domed courthouse looming at one end. There's a sock hop going on outside, with '50s-style outfits and antique cars tooling around. Here and there are a few brawny and bearded Southern country boys—much like myself—I'd like to rope and ride just as I did Trey, but, of course, they're all accompanied by cheap-looking, plump women in too-tight outfits, leading around noisy passels of brats. Oddly, on every other street corner, there are bear statues, painted in various garish colors. The town mascot? Whatever the reason, it's a funny irony. John takes a picture of me posing beside one that has PLEASE DON'T FEED across its chest.

Dinnertime. We settle into an Irish pub, taking a table by the front window. The waitress is as friendly and mannerly as I'd expect, her accent as Southern-bred as mine. The music's loud, stuff from the '70s and '80s, back when I was young, when I was a horny cub like Trey, when my beard was still black. John orders chicken potpie; I order fish and chips. We down a few brews, watch the plethora of straight folks stroll by outside.

I know this world, the small-town South. It's my world too. I know the landscape, the way catalpa blooms this time of year, and elderberry bushes, white as sea foam along the creek. Sprawling, sweet honeysuckle, and magnolias, with waxy petals and heavy, lemony scent. And starry rock lilies, on abandoned homesteads and overgrown graveyards. A damned church every quarter of a mile, and kudzu festering over the hillsides, swallowing broken barns and split-rail fences, and mockingbirds chattering among perfumed pink powder puffs of mimosa. And kinky good ole boys like me, giving the finger to fundamentalists, meeting men in what spaces we can, binding their hands and feet, gagging their handsome mouths, sucking their cocks, riding their eager asses, chewing their hairy tits and pits, lapping their bearded chins, doing whatever our bodies desire.

I grin. I rub the C.S.A. tattoo etched in swirls of black flame on my left shoulder. "To the South," I say, smiling, lifting my beer mug. John cocks a dubious eyebrow but knocks mugs with me anyway. I take a swig, sit back and wait for the food to arrive. Brushing my beard, I smell Trey's faint musk, lingering still on my fingertips.

TOM'S FEET

Gregory L. Norris

I

It's raining outside. I'm sitting in our room, thinking and wishing how mean, how evil, Tom really isn't, when I look up and he's standing at the bedroom door. He's dressed in his uniform and a pair of dirty sweat socks, sans his big police boots. I feel the gravitational pull from his feet, tugging at my eyes. Tom has the sexiest feet of any man alive, I'm convinced. I fall under their power for the thousandth, millionth time and realize we're both villains. Me, because I love and loathe him, both in the same breath.

Him, because he's sweet and mean, big and dumb, ugly and handsome, all at the same time. It's like ten different people occupying one body. And also because he took off his boots and is peeling off those dirty socks, the toes gray with perspiration, baring his big, masculine feet and knowing I'll be hypnotized by the image. Tom, now barefoot, his giant sweaty feet exposed at the cuffs of his black uniform pants, scratches at his balls.

They're quite the pair of above-average body parts, too, like his magnificent size-twelves.

"What's your problem?" he asks.

"No problem."

He growls, his voice a basic baritone, "What then?"

I draw in a breath before answering, smelling *him* on it: the warm, buttery odor of Tom's feet, the clean scent of his male sweat, fresh and exciting, from the rest of his body. Once, he told me that good people see Satan hiding around every corner, while bad people who do unthinkable acts of violence find God in prison. "Devil," I say.

"Huh?"

"Nothing," I lie. "I was just trying to understand how we got here."

He unzips his pants, goes fishing in his boxer-briefs, blue ones, dark navy. His nuts hang full and swollen beneath the tube-shaped impression of his dick. "I don't know, but I can tell you *where* we're going."

He lifts up his black uniform shirt and the white T-shirt beneath, baring the fur-ringed O of his belly button and the treasure trail of hair that cuts him down the center of his muscled abdomen, connecting the crossbar of pelt on his chest to the lush curls sprouting out of the top of his waistband. His body matches his feet. Tom is so attractive, with his cold blue eyes; his neat, dark hair in its athlete's cut, going silver just above the ears; the five o'clock shadow around a trim mustache that loves to tickle me in places no other tongue was ever allowed to venture; it sometimes *hurts* to look at him directly.

"Cut the shit," he says. "I'm horny."

"You're always horny."

"Lucky you."

"Lucky me?"

"Yeah, I saved you from a life of boredom and bad sex. Now how about you suck my cock."

I wince, scowl.

"Okay, start with my feet if you want. They should be hot and stinky, just the way you love them."

I shake my head. Just how the fuck *did* we get here?

I spotted him across the room. A man of his masculine attractiveness was impossible to miss. Dressed in jeans, a T-shirt, old hiking boots on huge feet, he scratched his back up and down against the wooden post, like a bear in the wild. Adding to that image, I heard him grunt. Those feet...on my way to the lodge's front desk, I imagined how sexy they must be in those well-traveled boots, warm and sweaty, exuding the scent of a real man. I felt eyes wandering over me and looked back up to see that I was being studied in return.

The bear ambled over. A chill tumbled down my spine. He loomed behind me, tall enough to cast a shadow. All the moisture drained from my mouth.

"Single?" he growled, washing a warm breath down my neck.

I tipped a glance over my shoulder and caught a whiff of his scent: clean skin, masculine soap, minty toothpaste. "Excuse me?"

"You here for the singles weekend?"

A spring singles weekend at the Charlemont Lodge in the heart of the Berkshire Mountains, specifically for gay men. I was and told him so.

"Good. Walk with me."

To my surprise, I walked with the dude, out of the lodge's front door, along the flagstone path between the flower gardens and fruit trees.

"Name?" he asked. I told him. "Birthday?"

"What is this, a job application?" I countered playfully.

Grunting a laugh—I couldn't tell if there was any humor in that noise—he said, "Tom. I'm a cop now. Used to be in the army. I play softball in a league."

"Softball. Is that like baseball?" Tom nodded. "What's the difference?"

"Bigger balls," he said.

Our eyes met. I fell into the hypnotic power of his gaze. A cop? He was so handsome, so manly; I just couldn't place him as belonging in this landscape of rainbow flags and lonely hearts.

"You're gay?"

"I don't know," he said. "My last girlfriend was an inflate-a-mate."

"Hot," I chuckled. "So..."

"I'm horny. You're beautiful, even if you have a dick. What are you looking for?"

I stopped and narrowed my eyes. Was this dude for real? "I'll tell you what I'm not looking for—a man with too much gray matter. I'm talking he can't speak more than two syllables in a row. I want 'duh' to be a regular part of his vocabulary. I want a dumb bull. A stud who's a brain-dead zombie. We're talking Frankenstein, scars and all."

"I've got scars," Tom said. He flashed me the side of his right arm, where a long pale zipper cut across the flesh near his elbow for several inches, visible beneath threads of dark hair. "Got that one fighting Saddam's forces."

"Impressive. Neck bolts?"

"No bolts, but I got nuts. Big ones."

I boldly glanced down the front of his blue jeans. "So I see."

"Yeah, real softballs." He scratched at the meaty fullness between his legs.

My mouth watered. "That's the dumbest *and* sexiest pickup line I ever heard."

"Did it work?" he asked while yanking down his zipper.

"In spades. What are you doing?"

"Answer my question first. Why are you here?"

"I'm hunting for the buck with the biggest antlers. And I may have found him."

Tom flashed a dopey smile. I slipped my hand into his open fly. He was stiff. I gave his dick a squeeze.

"Oh, yes, the biggest set of horns..."

"That ain't a horn," Tom said.

"It'll do for honking."

He moved in close, circling his big feet around mine. He towered over me. "I want you."

"Clearly," I said, caressing his thickness through the warm cotton of his underwear. The mountains framed his magnificence. The magical springtime scent of the countryside mixed with Tom had me giddy. "I bet you have the sexiest feet," I said before I was able to censor the words.

"Feet?" he chuckled. "You into that?"

"Oh, yeah. How big are yours?"

"Twelves, and they stink."

"Even better," I whispered.

And then I dropped to my knees in front of him and freed his dick and nuts from his underwear. Tom's cock snapped up, a modestly average, upward-curved and thick tube above two bigger-than-average balls, all of it wreathed in dark scruff.

I went down on Tom among the fruit trees, apple and cherry and peach with their necklaces of sweet-smelling blossoms, and, for the first time ever, I allowed a man to eat my asshole. That cop's mustache had, by all accounts, gotten plenty of experience licking out pussy. It brought me to a near-violent climax for the first of what would amount to at least a dozen times outside of and upstairs in the Charlemont Lodge.

I start with his feet, caressing them, sniffing them, looping my tongue in figure eights around his sweaty toes. Tom's foot odor, to me, is narcotic. I'm addicted to it, to him. He's a basic man, but also a complex one—he likes sports, he works the ultimate he-man's job, and he's handsome...so incredibly handsome.

But there are also layers to him that others don't see, and he probably isn't aware of himself. The one that can be childish and cruel for no good reason, like when we're in bed watching TV and I say something and Tom explodes.

"Shhh!"

"Don't *shhh* me."

"Cut it out. I can't hear the TV, *ass-hole*."

Ass-hole is one of Tom's favorites. He has a way of stressing both syllables, breaking the one word into two. Hey, all those years ago, I asked for a man with a limited vocabulary of grunts and groans, and I got him.

Tom's feet, a decade after we met that weekend at the Charlemont Lodge, are as sexy now as they were then. He clips his toenails. Though he still plays sports and has throughout his entire life, spent four years in the military and is a cop, he's taken great care of them. They sweat. They stink. The feet of a real man: I've often wondered if Tom's feet are the real reason we've stayed together for so long. I love men's feet and know that after worshipping at the best, all others would be a letdown. And Tom loves having me there, kneeling low before him, part of that complexity I've already alluded to. The yin and the yang. Top and bottom. Cop and writer. Tom and me.

He doesn't know about the bag I packed during his duty shift. He doesn't suspect I'm going to leave him.

II

My boyfriend Tom saws logs in the bedroom of our house on Sawyer Avenue. Can a man you've lived with for ten years still be your boyfriend, or after seven are you legally, socially and morally bound to something bigger? Husband? Soul mate? Curse? If I leave him, do I get something like alimony? What would they call that, for gay men, if it exists? *Swallimony?*

Tom snores, one giant bare foot and length of hairy athlete's leg hanging out from the covers. He's flat on his spine. One hand under the blanket has a choke hold on his junk. The temptation to crawl underneath and wrap my mouth around the place where his fingers squeeze nearly overwhelms me. But if I wake him, I might never leave, and I've been leaving Tom in my heart and in my mind for some time now, only he keeps pulling me back through spells and sorcery.

I resist looking at his foot. Tom has the most amazing feet, size-twelves, a real man's feet, as I've already told you. Earlier in the night, following his duty shift at the station, I worshipped Tom's feet for almost an hour. And, as has happened so often in our ten-year romance, my sniffing and licking his sweaty toes drove his cock to bust a particularly large load, which I happily lapped up. Tom shoots big, always has. Once, years ago, a stray rope of his seed flew clear over my head and hit the lampshade. Neither of us realized sperm is a natural bleaching agent until he switched the lamp on, later that night. For several years, that snakelike swirl was a constant reminder of how well we worked together, him a handsome, macho beat cop; me, an effeminate, moderately successful writer with a fetish for men's feet, and the best set on the planet only one room away.

I don't go back into the bedroom. Instead, I reach into the closet, behind the winter coats and Tom's sports gear, and pull out the suitcase and my briefcase, both of which are packed with the essentials. If I went back, I'd see his legs...*fuck*, Tom has such great legs. His feet, too. I'd lick my way up to his balls, which had ridden my chin not seven hours earlier, and suck his cock and swallow his potent swimmers down, and be impregnated by him as much as one male, dominant, could the other, submissive. And I would never leave.

I grip my car keys and creep toward the front door. *Creep*, being the operative word.

On May 26, 1994, the Hubbell Space Telescope discovered concrete proof of the existence of black holes. The same day, I uncovered concrete proof of *ass-holes*, thanks to my new boyfriend Tom.

"Would you put the damn book down?" he grumbled.

We'd fucked twice that Saturday afternoon alone, in my room at the Charlemont Lodge. His thickness was still a phantom presence in my ass, a memory of tingles and the rough, sweaty slap of his balls against my butt. "No," I said dryly.

"Only fags read."

"Only a fag would know that," I fired back.

Tom yanked the sheet aside and stormed out of bed, his erect dick metronoming from side to side over two hairy, low-hanging balls.

"Where are you going?" I asked.

"To fuck your father."

"Say hi to dad for me," I said, no trace of my building anger detectable. "So this is it, huh? You're breaking up with me after...a day, now, is it?"

"I'm fucking horny," he said, brooding.

"Well, good if you are, because I don't want to be tied down...just tied up, you bonehead."

He reached for his underwear, a pair of gray boxer-briefs that looked so good on him, they should have been criminal. Tom winced as his thickness was jammed under cover. "Fuck you."

"You wish."

"Yeah, obviously. You're the hottest fucking piece of ass I've ever laid eyes on, *ass-hole.*"

He started toward the door, but stopped, chuckling with his back turned to me. I laughed, too. We fucked. Our first breakup, one of so many that weekend and in the years that followed, was forgotten, setting an unhealthy tone. You can't draw lines in the sand only to laugh loud enough to blow them away. If you do, you end up with some dude who loves to fuck you, but you'll be fucked to know if he really loves you.

The fine folks at the Charlemont Lodge had decorated the joint in pride flags and a pink triangle windsock. They'd booked the place almost to capacity, according to the buzz in the restaurant downstairs, but you didn't see it based on the distance between elbows at the bar—which I'd guessed meant there were far fewer singles by Saturday night than there had been on Friday afternoon.

I had seen the car in the parking lot. Hard to miss a cherry-red sports car with *C-Men* for a vanity license plate. The owner of the car was a dirty blond with a tight caboose, dressed in jeans and loafers, no socks. I'd had zero interest in licking his toes even before meeting Tom. He was too much like me, too polished, too much of a swish. I'd snuck out of bed after caving to Tom's demands and was down at the bar's acre of dark wood, nursing a cranberry martini, when C-Men sidled over.

"Hey," he said.

"Hey," I answered.

It was late, and some of the missing persons, who'd been holed up fucking, like me, had returned to the public eye for late-night drinks and munchies. He ordered a white wine. He was too close to me.

"Get any?"

"I've gotten too much," I said.

He mewled out a lusty sigh. "Fantastic for you. I know someone staying in the carriage house that got fucked up the ass with a grape Popsicle. He's gonna shit purple for a week."

I resisted the urge to laugh—why encourage unwanted attentions?

"So, what's your name?" he asked.

"Curtis," I lied.

"Hey, Curt. Oh, shit, there's that dude!"

I sipped my drink. "The Popsicle?"

"Hell, no. Big macho stud I saw yesterday. Ain't seen much of him since. Probably one of those *faux-mosexuals*. You know, a straight dude just looking to get his rocks off. Still, I wouldn't mind swimming in his gene pool." C-Men rolled his eyes. "I'd like to see him coming around my mountain when I come."

I ignored him. He elbowed me. "What?"

"Ever see that old Charlton Heston movie, *Planet of the Apes*?" He extended a finger secretively toward the restaurant's arched entrance. I followed it. There stood Tom.

He was in a T-shirt, black shorts, old jogging sneakers, minus socks. Seeing his legs and bare ankles sent my heart into a gallop.

"Hello, daddy," C-Men hissed, taking another sip. "That's the guy!"

Tom's worried expression triggered something inside me that I hadn't thought possible. True, I'd been giddy at having sex with so incredible a man; I'd even felt that illusory rush of intense emotion that masquerades as love, but is really only the molecules of intense orgasms exploding into a localized reenactment of the Big Bang that first gave life to the universe. Real love is born when you see concern written across another person's face, and your heart aches in response.

"He's coming over," C-Men whispered. "Just so you understand, he's mine."

"No, that's where you're wrong," I said. "That ape's *mine*."

I slid off the bar stool. "Tom."

"I woke up and you were gone, dude," he grumbled. "Is everything okay?"

"Everything's perfect," I said.

Tom cast a wary glance around the restaurant. Every eye was on us. On *him*, more accurately—he looked great. But he only saw me. "I'm pissed at you," he said. "You freaked me out."

"Well, that makes two of us, bonehead," I countered. "Come on, let's get out of here."

"Yeah, but just so you know, you owe me, and I plan to collect," he said. "I'll take a hum-job, for starters."

I sighed a swear under my breath, hooked my smaller arm around his, and we headed back to Tom's room, where I promptly made it up to him, starting at those incredible feet, which had grown sweaty in their stinky old sneakers.

It was a hell of a weekend. We moved in together less than a month later.

I shove my shit into the backseat and carefully close the door. My little car's parked on the other side of Tom's nutcracker of a truck, but no sound carries like a slamming car door, and though the dude's a heavy sleeper, I don't want him to wake up. A toe job followed by a deep rim job and a balls-deep blow job have left my boyfriend of ten years crashed out and snoring. But Tom's a cop. If he hears the car door shut, he'll be awake and in pursuit. I'm a coward and it's better this way. He's a handsome man. The handsomest. He'll find an endless supply of dudes to fill the small void I'll leave behind. Ladies, too, most likely. Two nights ago, I caught him jacking off to lesbian porn on the Internet. I guess he's straighter than he's led me to believe since we met a decade ago in the Berkshires.

I love Tom, but I'm adult enough now to understand that love isn't always enough. Especially when the dude you love thinks sex is the definition of the emotion.

Tom doesn't love me. He loves my mouth and my 'pussy'—his name for my asshole. Sitting behind the wheel, my pussy tingles from the insatiable hunger his mouth and mustache (and then his dick) showed it, mere hours earlier.

I glance at our home, a modest house perfect for two, and hesitate. The ghostly glare of the TV is visible upstairs, in our room, where he sleeps. The memory of Tom's feet paralyzes me. There's been so much sex, so many moments spent worshipping at those big, handsome feet...if I never have sex again, the memories will suffice, I tell myself. They'll have to.

I put the car in reverse, back out, shift to DRIVE, and go.

III

It's just after two in the morning. I've just broken up with my hunky cop boyfriend of ten years, Tom; only he doesn't realize it yet. I'm at an all-night diner perched on a waterfall that I've always wanted to visit, but never got around to until now.

We had a great fight two days ago. Tom and I have some hilarious spats that are too good to not write about and, being a writer, I've often pulled material from them. Most of our fights start with Tom not getting his way, not giving an inch, and forgetting that I've got a fifty-percent say in the matters of our life together.

This one went something like this:

Me: "Movie? I'd like to see some Fellini."

Tom: "You would, would you? Well, I'd prefer some *fellatio*."

He grabbed his junk and gave it a shake. He was standing in a pair of blue jeans; a T-shirt ripped under one arm that showed the dark nest of his pit fur, an old baseball cap, bill pointing forward. No socks. Blue jeans and bare feet. Heavenly distraction!

For some time, Tom has used that part of his anatomy to get his way. The manipulative prick has the sexiest pair of giant sweaty dogs and, knowing I have a mean foot fetish, uses it to his advantage. On that particular afternoon, he'd gone out to the driveway to shoot hoops and had conveniently left off his socks, knowing the stinky old pair of high-tops would bake his toes in that buttery aroma, and I'd be powerless to resist anything he demanded of me.

He was right and knew he would win.

"I'm fucking horny," he moaned.

"From shooting hoops?"

Tom's balls are always swelling up, sagging low and needing release after his police softball league, or pickup football with the guys, or the hockey team he joined two winters ago because he was, to quote, "bored and waiting for Spring Training to begin." Half an hour of shooting the basketball at the hoop shouldn't have made that much of a difference, but clearly it did.

"I want to watch that movie," I said.

"Tape it."

"How about you hold on for a few hours and I'll lick you senseless then."

"Can't."

"Then go upstairs and touch yourself in that oh-so-private way."

I started to walk away. Tom pulled me into his arms and humped against me, his cock at full mast, still trapped inside his jeans. "I'd much rather that *you* play with it. My feet are hot and smelly, just the way you love them."

"Love?" I chuckled. "How about you show me a little and let me watch my damn foreign film."

That pissed him off. Being denied always does. "Fine," he huffed, and I knew he was about to have the six-foot-three, thirty-five-year-old man's version of a young boy's tantrum. "I did it for you."

"Did what?"

"Got my body ready in the way that turns you on."

"You're always turned on."

"Not right now, I'm not." He pushed me away and grabbed the hardcover copy of a historical war novel he was reading off the kitchen counter. "I'm going upstairs. When you're ready to apologize, I'll be reading my book."

He was acting like a child, and I wasn't in the mood. "That won't take you long. Why don't I recite it for you so you don't have to strain your eyes? 'See Spot run...'"

Tom fixed me with his cold blue eyes. "Yeah, well if it was a book you'd written, it would say, 'See John fuck Spot.'"

"If you'd written it—factoring in, of course, *if you can even write*—it would read, 'See Tom fuck Jill while secretly fucking John and Spot.'"

"Fuck you."

"You wish."

"We've already established that, *ass-hole*."

He blew a fart with his mouth and plodded up the stairs. Real mature. I tracked those amazing bare feet up the risers, and the itch they always unleash in that part of my DNA that's attracted to Tom's feet ignited.

Ten minutes later, I wandered upstairs, intending to give him what he wanted. I caught Tom jacking off at his computer, as suspected. He was watching Jill fuck another Jill and told me to not let the door hit my ass on the way out.

And then it struck me that Tom had never really loved me, just my mouth and what I did to him with it.

This past winter, Tom and I returned to the Charlemont Lodge. He'd accrued a week of sick time and was going to lose it if he didn't use it. We rented the carriage house out back, which came with its own fireplace and a pool table. We skied for a day at one of the nearby slopes. Mostly, we fucked.

The world ten years earlier had been a vastly different place. Cell phones weren't clamped to every ear. There were no social networking sites, no Internet to speak of. The Charlemont Lodge had changed. They offered WiFi in the lobby now. The pride flags were gone. The restaurant had gotten a makeover and looked brighter and fresher, but something had been lost in sprucing up all that dark wood.

With relative ease, Tom built a fire in the fireplace.

"Something they teach you in the army," he said, dressed only in a pair of long johns. The rest of his ski clothes were draped over the backs of chairs, drying. His big feet looked remarkably warm and pink, sticking out of the cuffs of his crisp white bottoms. I stole a glance at his naked back. How often had I followed the pattern of freckles on his shoulders, connecting the dots with kisses?

He studied the fire, his eyes captured by the flames. I studied Tom. He was all fire, but few clues. Those shoulders...those *feet*. Had almost ten years really passed between our first encounter at the Charlemont Lodge and this one? For an instant, I was looking at Tom with new eyes. He turned to see me smiling and smiled, too. I slid over to him, cupped his unshaved chin, and kissed him full on the lips. Tom's cock pulsed in his long johns. I reached down and gave it a tug. His balls felt full and sweaty.

"Having fun?" he growled.

"Oh, very much so."

I slid down and took his thickness between my lips. The funky male musk earned from hours on the slopes sparked on my taste buds and burned in my nostrils, so arousing to me, so *Tom*. I licked his balls, which spilled out of the front flap.

"Yeah, suck on 'em, just like that," he commanded.

I dipped lower. I had to sniff his feet, taste them. I moaned his name and licked. Tom's cock leaked. He pulled me off his toes, spun me around and entered. While I was on all fours, he fucked me, grunting a blue streak of expletives.

"Gonna fuck that sweet ass...*fuck you doggy-style, dawg.*"

I giggled. "Doggy-style sounds so disgusting."

"Shut up and let me breed you, bitch."

"You know," I continued, nonplused, "some birds and insects do it the same way. Doesn't 'butterfly-style' sound so much prettier than doggy-style?"

In midthrust, Tom began to crack up behind me. He wrapped an arm around my waist and pulled me closer, riding me that way until both of us nutted and collapsed into the puddles of our mixed, mutual come.

"Butterfly-style," he sighed, nuzzling his face against mine. "You're fucking crazy."

We played pool, naked. I intentionally let Tom win.

"Minnesota Fats, I ain't," I said.

Tom leaned over to take a shot. I grabbed hold of his beaut of a butt. He scratched.

"Fucking *ass-hole*," he said lightly.

"You love it," I said, groping his balls. "Besides, you know my game's pocket pool."

He set down the pool stick, grabbed hold of me and boosted me up onto the pool table's felt top. While fucking me butterfly-style, Tom licked at my ears and whispered the words, in proper order.

"I love you..."

In the diner, my coffee sits untouched, long enough to have gone tepid. The knot in my stomach takes another violent twist. Tears sting at the corners of my eyes. What the fuck have I been thinking?

A sappy old song by the Captain & Tennille plays over the speakers. She croons about him being sunshine, shadow, morning, night; that he's hard times, he is good times, he's darkness and light.

I love Tom's feet. I love his cock. I love that scar on his arm, from the first Operation: Desert Storm. He's a pain in my ass. He's my hero.

I toss money on the table and hurry out of the diner, then speed home at ten miles above the posted speed limit, figuring that if I get pulled over Tom will fix the ticket. He always does.

Remembering that night in the Charlemont Lodge's carriage house puts everything back into perspective. He *does* love me. But Tom's a guy, a dude, a penis with feet...those sexy feet! And dudes don't always say it when it's easier to show.

Getting home seems to take forever. When I pull into the driveway, with a sinking heart I see that the living room light is on. Pulse racing, I walk in. Tom sits in his favorite chair, barefoot, bare-chested, wearing only his boxer-briefs. He flips channels on the TV but doesn't make eye contact.

"Something you want to tell me?" he asks.

"Yup. Here I am, asshole of the day yet again. Hope you'll forgive me, because I don't have room on the shelf for another trophy."

Not commenting, he demands to know where I've been.

"I went out for some air. I've been having trouble breathing the last few days."

Tom's eyes drift up and meet mine. "Pneumonia?"

"Naw, just one of those twenty-four-hour bugs. But it's passed. I feel much better now."

He gives me a tip of his chin, one of those typical Tom-dude-macho-guy gestures. "Good."

"Yeah, all better again."

"So, anything you want to tell me?" he presses.

"Only that I love you."

"That makes two of us. Always have, always will."

I mosey over to the recliner, slink down between his hairy legs and pull his big, handsome feet into my lap. All is well.

HOMECOMING

Jay Rogers

I stepped into the rust-stained concrete shower to wash the soot, dirt and sweat from my body. With the rest of the guys from the graveyard shift gone and the day shift already at their workstations, the squeak of the turning faucets echoed through an empty locker room. I began to scrub my skin clean but then stopped for a while to focus on the water flowing over my sore lats, biceps and quads. It was steaming, liquid rejuvenation. My soap-slicked hands glided over my pecs, stopping to circle each nipple before trailing down to roam the defined abs and lower crevices of my body, and before long I had focused on the one spot that really needed attention. Closing my eyes, I stroked my hardening cock until the last bit of lather streamed down my legs into the drain and the water began to run cold. The temperature change woke up my brain. It was a waste of time to stand here, jacking off—especially considering who was waiting at home. I toweled off before pulling on a T-shirt and cutoff sweats. The free swing of my cock and balls in the soft, loose fabric felt so great that I heartily enjoyed bagging my stiff, grimy uniform on the way out of the building.

The summer morning air landed on my chest like a pro wrestler executing a body slam. The heavy humidity held the smell of coal dust in the air and even seemed to dampen down the crunching sound of the gravel beneath my feet. *This is going to be a good day for indoor, air-conditioned activities,* I thought. Indoors. At home. It was difficult to remember what it was like to be home. Whenever the reservists who work at the power plant are called up to fight overseas, the remainder of the crew has to work overtime to keep power flowing to the city. I hadn't had a day off in over a month. Over the past thirty-two hours I had worked three eight-hour shifts with only eight hours off in between the first two. The last sixteen hours had been a blur. I was ready to properly enjoy the two days I would finally have off—courtesy of two very happy returning reservists. Part of my enjoyment was going to include Dan, who'd been working overtime as well and was now in bed at home.

I reached for the door of my truck. It creaked open. Spinning my hard hat across the seat, I climbed behind the wheel. The engine grumbled a bit before turning over, then steadily thumped away. The old hunk of steel shuddered as I threw it into gear and stepped on the gas. Although I empathized with its worn-out engine, the old Ford Apache could hardly move fast enough through the sweltering streets to suit me.

As I approached the one set of railroad tracks that divide this prairie town into eastern and western halves, lights flashed and crossing gates lowered. Swearing, I reluctantly rolled to a stop. Three chugging diesel-electrics emerged from the shimmering heat to lug a long chain of coal cars past the hood of the pickup. The heavy throb of the laboring engines pulsated through the oppressive air. *Whomp, whomp, whomp...* The oscillating vibrations worked their way through the thin, rusty floorboard beneath my feet, crept up my legs and then harmonized with the pulse of blood through my groin. Despite my exhaustion, the throbbing in my body grew, along with my cock. Pulsation after pulsation forged man flesh into a steel piston. I tempered the length of it with the palm of my hand, thinking again about Dan, waiting at home.

He worked in construction and did some remodeling jobs in between projects. Since he'd always gone easy on the beer, he had a hard body, from head to toe. God, until the first time I took his smooth head in my hands and slid my cock into his mouth, I never knew what great sex was about. We're not even sure how it all happened, that first time, because neither of us had ever thought of himself as gay. We'd always been friends but didn't really spend much time together until our kids had left home and we'd both gotten divorced. The bitter divorces gave us plenty in common, to begin with. Then we had my vintage truck and his GTO to keep running. In the winter, we took in sports on TV whenever we had free time. Being with Dan felt natural, I guess. One snowy night, after watching the Iowa wrestling team grope, grapple and pin a majority of the Michigan State guys, I suggested that Dan not go out into the storm. Maybe all the times we'd bumped elbows and knees, working under and around our vehicles, were leading up to it. Maybe it was just watching the body contact of the wrestlers that took us over the edge of whatever had been holding us back. Whatever it was, the moment he stepped out of his boots to stay the night, I grabbed the back of Dan's neck and pulled him into a kiss while he groped at my cock. After that, there wasn't a lot of talk about what it meant for us to be friends, then have sex, then live together. We just knew it was all right, somehow. What wasn't right was my sitting at this goddamn railroad crossing with a raging hard-on that should be filling Dan's warm, wet mouth.

The throbbing of the train eventually began to fade as I watched the FRED on the final car go by, but my blood was still pounding. When the crossing gates creaked and swayed to their upright position, I threw the Ford into gear and floored it. The engine roared with the flood of gasoline and the truck surged shakily over the tracks. My cock surged with blood and ached for Dan's talented mouth. He's always saying he can't get enough of my meat—that he loves going to work with a sore jaw, the taste of my jism on his tongue and the feeling of a well-fucked throat. I wasn't about to disappoint him. Precum seeped out of my piss slit and turned a growing spot on my sweats a deeper shade of gray. The drive home had never taken so long. The truck had hardly rolled to a stop before my feet hit the ground and the door clattered shut behind me.

I peeled off my T-shirt as I entered the kitchen. The air-conditioning felt good to my weary, overheated body, but the coolness did nothing to discourage my raging hard-on. By the light of the early sun filtering through the windows, I navigated the furniture obstacle course and reached the foot of the staircase, where I kicked off my shoes. The wooden treads chilled my bare feet as I lightly took the steps two at a time. I shucked my shorts at the top of the stairs. Stiff dick swaying with every step, I entered the bedroom and quietly moved through the shadows. The outline of my lover was sprawled diagonally across the bed. The sight of him on his back with his arms over his head cranked up the urgency in my groin. *Perfect,* I thought, *so fucking perfect.*

Dan barely stirred when my right knee sank into the mattress. He only mumbled when I threw the other leg over his chest. His features were relaxed, motionless, as my engorged limb bobbed over his face in time to my heartbeat. So close to his hot siphon of a mouth, my desire oozed out of my piss slit in a glistening drop of precum that stretched closer to Dan's face with every pulse. Despite my impatience, I wanted to ease into his throat. I wanted him to be fully awake so that he could enjoy this as much as I was going to enjoy it. I lowered myself down onto his chest, allowing the dripping tip of my dick to bounce lightly on Dan's lips. A white-hot bolt of lust burned down my dick and jolted my body.

Even in his sleep, Dan was ready. His tongue snaked out to lick my precum pearls a second before his eyes fluttered open. I was not able to hold back any longer. "Good morning," I growled, taking his smoothly shaven head in my hands. Dan groaned and his lips parted. I shifted my weight forward. His hot trap closed around my cock and his hands reached for my ass, so I began to thrust into the slick warmth of his mouth. His tongue sleepily slithered along the sensitive underside of my cock, making the ball sac at the base of my seven inches churn. But Dan was beginning to wake up, and the growing suction he put on my shaft sent another bolt of lust burning through my body. He looked up to enjoy the grimace of agonizing pleasure that must have shown on my face but then closed his eyes—in concentration this time, not sleep—and his hands tightened their grip on my ass to pull me deeper into his mouth.

"Oh, yeah," I encouraged him, "that's it. Suck it." Driving it down again and again, I worked my cockhead into the sucking depths. When my meat hit the back of Dan's mouth and slid down his throat I groaned, "Uh, shit!" The suction, tongue and massaging throat action were so intense that I slapped my palms up against the wall behind the bed to brace myself. I was losing track of everything besides my aching shaft. I had to keep on pile driving, to fuck my lover's throat deeper and deeper. I became all cock. Electrified, ready-to-bust pleasure was all I experienced. I barely noticed the muffled groaning and slurping noises Dan was making as he sucked down my burgeoning dick, thrust after thrust. Time seemed suspended until my balls clenched up tight and started pumping spunk. "Fuck...aw, fuck!" I shoved my cock halfway to Dan's stomach as satisfaction exploded through my piss slit in waves, waves that fed Dan his first meal of the day.

The suction let up and Dan's mouth opened in a guttural howl just as I felt warm ropes of cum hit my back. He came without touching himself—proof positive that Dan loved my cock. In fact, his lips closed back on the softening flesh to suck out the last drops of cum. I reluctantly pulled back and rolled off my lover, who turned onto his side to put his arm around me. The satisfaction and exhaustion were overwhelming. Drifting off to sleep, I thought, *Now that's what I call a workingman's homecoming.*

RINGS

R. J. Bradshaw

The claddagh ring on his left hand: that's all he's wearing when I get home from work. He stands with perfect posture in the hallway, a seductive smirk on his face.

"Nice outfit," I comment, my eyes indulging in him as I close the door behind me and kick off my shoes. My dick is already growing, as is my curiosity. I don't know what I did, but I must've done something right.

The silver ring is reflecting light from the kitchen. In our five years, he's never taken it off. I glance down at my own ring, identical to his; even the sizing is the same. The romantic in him had insisted that we get a matching pair, "because our hearts match," he said. I've never been the sappy type, but I like that; it makes sense to me. *We* make sense to me.

"These old rags?" he scoffs, pretending to brush dust from his naked skin. "I've had these *forever*. I found them stashed away under a pile of clothes."

"Turn around," I prompt. "I wanna check you out from all angles."

He raises his arms and does a slow three-sixty. Five years have added a few more grays to his coarse brown hair and some pudge to his midsection, but everything else is the same. At ninety degrees, I take in the familiar profile of his face: the wisp of his eyelashes, the curves of his nose and chin, his rosy lips. At one-eighty, he models his broad and freckled shoulders, the patch of hair on his lower back and the tiny birthmark on his right buttcheek. At two-seventy, my gaze follows the arch of his back down to the convex of his ass and then across to his thick cock; it's somewhere between flaccid and erect: not resting against his sac, but not pointing at the ceiling either. Scanning farther down, I focus on the definition in his legs and feet, the muscles flexing slightly with each small movement of his turn.

My dick has fully stiffened and is in desperate need of repositioning. He catches me adjusting myself as he comes around to face me again, delighted by the effect he's had on me. This is my favorite angle of him: full frontal...dark twinkling eyes, impish smile, hairy muscled chest, knobby knees and a beautiful cock. Sex usually happens with the lights out, so it's been about two weeks since I've looked at him this closely: far too long. How can someone so familiar still fascinate me this much and still get me this hard?

"Is that what you're wearing to the restaurant?" I question. I'm trying to be funny, but the delivery is all wrong; he's too distracting.

Tuesday is our night to eat out; we always hit the fifties-style diner on Circle Drive, pop coins in the old jukebox and eat pancakes drowned in syrup. Breakfast for supper: a guilty pleasure that we have in common.

"We're staying in tonight," he replies, stepping toward me. I'm still standing in front of the door. After walking in to find him naked, it never crossed my mind that I could move. "Don't worry," he adds, knowingly. "There's a casserole in the oven."

I sniff the air. "The cheesy kind?" I ask expectantly.

"Of course."

He's now close enough to kiss me, but he doesn't. I can smell the sweetness on his breath and his freshly washed skin. His arms are hanging beside him; he wants me to initiate contact, and I gladly oblige. I raise my hands to each of his bristled cheeks, my lips moving to his, my tongue sliding inside his mouth. He unzips my jacket, yanking my arms down to strip it off. Wasting no time, he pulls my T-shirt over my head, creating only a brief interruption in our kiss. Suddenly, I feel his arms around me, warm hands on my back and his bare stomach pressed against mine; our erections dig into each other's waist, one naked and one clothed.

He's kissing my neck when I spit in my palm. Reaching down, I take hold of his huge dick, using my saliva to jack him off.

"Don't," he whispers in my ear, taking my hand from his cock. "This time it's all about *you*."

"But I like to..."

"Next time," he promises. He wants to be in charge, and I'm not about to stop him.

"Bedroom?" I ask.

"Couch is closer."

His fingers grasp the band of my pants and, stepping backward, he jerks me into the living room. Pushing me down on the cushions, he rapidly unbuttons my jeans and tugs them down my legs, past my knees and feet and onto the floor. He peels off one sock and then the other, throwing them behind him; all I have left is my claddagh ring and my underwear, a wet precum spot where the tip of my dick lies hidden.

"What's gotten into you tonight?" I question, half laughing, half panting. It's not like we never have sex; we have sex frequently, but he's not usually this...eager. I'm reminded of ringing church bells and the hot fuck that followed. He was dominant that night too. I enjoy that.

"Life is too short to spend another hour without your cock in my mouth," he states.

Whether he realizes it or not, he gets into these "life is too short" kicks about once a month, and I'm always excited for the next one. Sometimes we go out dancing or get a room at a five-star hotel. Sometimes we dress up and dine at some swanky restaurant or skip a day of work to lie in bed. In January we booked a couple of plane tickets. And then sometimes...

When he removes my briefs, he doesn't tear them off as I expected. He lifts the fabric from my dick, revealing only the head at first. He spends several seconds licking it, savoring my precum. Very slowly, his tongue follows my underwear as it shifts farther down, over my shaft and scrotum and the space beneath. I can't imagine anything feeling better. And then, as my briefs slip past my knees, he wraps his lips around my cock. He inhales and exhales through his nose, my erection coasting in and out of his mouth. His right hand grips my shaft, pumping it and sucking it in unison, pace quickening with each stroke.

"Whoa," I breathe, urging him to decelerate. "You're gonna make me come..."

He releases my dick from his lips. "Don't you dare," he asserts with a grin. "I wanna fuck you before this is done. You up for that?"

"Do you need to ask?" He doesn't. He knows how much I love it when he tops me, but he's not usually in the mood.

"Be right back," he says, bounding upstairs, cock bouncing.

I finger my asshole while he's gone, prepping for him, the

anticipation nearly killing me. I can't believe that this is going to happen. It's been weeks since I played the catcher.

"I bought you something," he reports, sauntering down the stairs.

"You're full of surprises tonight," I remark.

He tosses a small rubber circlet on my chest.

"Oh...thanks," I say, holding it up to get a good look at it. I have no idea what it's supposed to be.

"It's a cock ring," he chortles, obviously aware of my confusion.

"A cock ring?"

"Yeah, so you don't go limp when I'm fucking you."

That does tend to happen.

I fiddle with the black ring, gauging its size and testing its elasticity, wondering how the hell I'm supposed to get it around my cock and balls. "It's a bit *small*, don't you think?"

He's having a giggle attack. "I got the kind that fits the shaft only."

"Oh, I didn't know they made those." Interested, I inspect the ring again.

"Well..." he prompts. "Try it on."

My dick has softened slightly, so it seems like a good time to test it out. Using saliva as lubricant, I slide it on easily, over my head and down my shaft to the base. I masturbate to get my full hard-on back; the ring feels tighter as my cock swells, but I think it's supposed to, and it's not uncomfortable.

"Huh. Fits pretty good," I say.

"I showed the clerk what my lips look like when I suck it, and she told me which size to get." He never ceases to amaze me with his ingenuity.

"How do you want me?" I ask.

"On your stomach. I wanna fuck you from behind." I've

never heard him use the word *fuck* this frequently. It gets me even hornier, if that's possible.

When I flip onto my front, he gets on top, placing his legs on each side of me. I raise my backside to him and he massages the ring of my ass with the tip of his cock, moistening it with his precum. His head stretches my hole as he begins to enter me, causing me to gasp as he pushes farther. I should have prepped with something bigger than a finger; his girth is almost too much for my tight ass to handle.

"Relax," he whispers, and I listen, unclenching my ass to let him in.

He kisses my back and his cock advances, all the way; his sac and pubic hair brush my skin, his erection pokes my prostate. He pulls back gradually before pushing into me again, caressing my inner walls with his shaft. He speeds the motion, gliding in and out as I bite my lip in pleasure.

And then the telephone rings.

"Honey, can you get that?" I joke.

"Would you shut up?" he replies teasingly, lunging in as deep as he can. On a normal day, nothing would have stopped him from answering it; he tends to be paranoid about emergencies.

The phone rings three more times, followed by the sound of heavy breathing and the slapping of skin against skin. His thick shaft brings stinging ecstasy with each thrust, a moan escaping my throat whenever it touches my gland. The cock ring is doing its job, my erection still complete when he reaches around to grab it. He starts to jack me off as he fucks me. He pounds me hard, and then harder, his hips slamming into me, his sweat dripping onto my back.

"I'm gonna co…" he squeaks, his body convulsing on top of me, his hot semen spilling in my ass. It feels so fucking incredible.

"Keep going," I sigh. "I'm almost there..."

He loses momentum, but continues to fuck me, trembling with the effort. My hand relieves his, masturbating as his fat dick slides inside me. Within moments I'm coming, my semen spraying all over the couch.

"Holy shit," I pant, my chest heaving.

I twitch as he pulls out, rolling off of me with a burst of exhilarated laughter.

"We should do that more often," he proposes, his hand running through my hair.

I can't even speak; I can barely comprehend what just happened. That was the best sex we've had in ages and well worth the wait. Shifting onto my side, I look into his shining eyes. We let minutes pass in contented silence, cuddled into each other, lying in a puddle of cum. I take his left hand into mine, our claddagh rings nearly touching.

"Do you realize," I chuckle, "that we're wearing matching outfits? In thirty years, we'll be just like that old couple down the street."

"The speed walkers with the blue jumpsuits?"

"Yup."

He glances down at our hands. "I don't think that wearing matching wedding rings is really the same thing," he giggles. "But maybe."

"I would be okay with that. Just so you know."

He smiles; it's not the usual devilish grin, but an expression of fulfillment, of love.

"Are you hungry?" he asks, his warm body rising from mine.

"For your cheesy casserole?" I respond. "Always."

He winks back at me before rounding the corner, spanking his pale bare ass for my amusement.

"Coming right up."

I rest my head on a pillow and start planning for Thursday, my day off work; I'm already looking forward to returning the favors.

SKYROCKETS IN FLIGHT

Rob Rosen

My morning had started off mighty shitty, with meetings on top of meetings, which was why the email put such a smile on my face—oh, and a lump in my slacks, crowbar thick and megastiff. A stunning guy on all fours radiated from my screen, ass to the camera, pink hole winking, hair rimmed and ready for poking. I jumped up and locked my office door, window slats shut good and tight, phone off the hook, before slinging on my headset and booting up my Skype.

"I think I know that hole," I purred into the microphone.

"It says hello," came the chuckled reply. "And it's waiting for you." I watched as he reached around and slid a slicked-up finger inside, its neighbor joining the fray, the lens zooming in for a close-up. Yu-fucking-um.

I unzipped my fly and released the beast, seven steely inches springing out, leaking copious amounts of jizz. I gave it a tug and a squeeze, then a stroke, then another. "It's the middle of the day, Jack," I groaned.

His hand retracted, then shoved on in again, out, in, the noise like a squishy symphony. "'Skyrockets in flight,'" he sang, all AM-radio-like, in between grunts.

"'Afternoon delight,'" I sang back, finishing the refrain, my balls rising at the very thought of what he had in mind. And then I noticed something: The bed. The sheets. Even the wall. "Where the fuck are you?" I rasped, already coaxing the come up from my balls.

He swung around, handsome face pointed my way. "That's for me to know and you to find out."

I stood up and smacked my cock against the lens, his mouth opening wide, eager to take me in, pixel by glorious pixel. "Treasure hunt, huh?" I asked, one part curious, two parts horny as all fuck.

"Get here quick enough and it'll be *buried* treasure, Rick," he groaned, winking at me, the image pulling back, widening, his massive cock swaying between his thick thighs as he continued to work his hole from behind. "Better hurry, though; Vesuvius is about to erupt." And with that, the screen went black, an email suddenly appearing in my inbox in its stead.

I rested my still-throbbing cock on the desk, a trickle of precome glistening on the polished maple. "Multiply the number of years we've been together by the length of my dangling left nut," I read aloud off the screen. "Then you're halfway there."

I ran my finger through the sticky desk-spunk before sucking it off, the salty sweetness hitting my throat like a bullet. "Eight years," I whispered. "Eight years together." I smiled and shoved my semiwoody back in my slacks. "And his left nut hangs six inches down low. A half an inch farther than the right." Which we'd measured in year number three. "Eight times six is forty-eight." I scratched my head and headed out of my office, my assistant, Beth, staring up at me from her desk.

"Off to your afternoon lunch meeting, Rick?" she asked.

A flush of crimson spread from ear to ear. "Um, cancel it." I shifted my cock down, the bulge only slightly less noticeable. "Something suddenly came up."

She sighed and began typing lightning fast across her keyboard. "Done. Anything I can do to help?"

The flush burnt hot down my neck. "Forty-eight is halfway to what, Beth?"

She tilted her head to the side and squinted at me. "Ninety-six, Rick. Why?"

I coughed and tapped my foot, eager to get going, even more eager to be slamming my way inside of him. "That have any meaning to you? Any address that stands out? Locations with that number?"

Her eyes closed, her brain clearly Rolodexing. She smiled and popped them back open. "Hotel Ninety-Six, three blocks from here. Fancy digs." Again she began to type. "Five stars on Yelp. Better not let Jack catch you there," she chided, a wagging finger pointed my way.

If she only knew, I thought. *Better yet, maybe not.*

"Um, nothing like that. Be back in a couple. Cover for me." I ran out. Then back in. "Please." Then back out again, superfast, cock already thickening, balls bouncing as I took the stairs two at a time, three, my heart beating a mile a minute now.

I made it to my car in no time flat, flinging the door open and then hopping in, my hubby clearly one step ahead of me. The paper sat on the passenger seat, another surprise resting just beneath. *Put these on,* the note read. *You'll need them later.*

I held the nipple clamps up for closer inspection, the thin metal connecting chain swinging down, a sizzle of adrenal suddenly riding shotgun down my spine, a trickle of sweat streaming down my forehead. "Fucker," I moaned, turning my head from side to side, making sure I wasn't in anybody's line of sight. Then I unbuttoned my shirt, my hand running through the dense matting of fur, and tweaked my right nipple, the flesh pulsing to life; ditto the left one, both of them ready and waiting now.

Panting, I clipped the toy on, pain mixing with abject pleasure in just under a second, a warm eddy rippling through my belly as I once again popped my prick out. I bent over while my iPhone snapped away, my cock pinning the chain to my chest, nipples already beet red and throbbing in delight. Then I hit SEND.

He replied lickety-split. "Good boy. Now hurry. X marks the spot."

I gave a tug on the chain, every nerve ending in my body suddenly on fire, my cock ready to explode. Still, once again I shoved it back in and then tore out of the parking lot, my tires squealing in protest. Thankfully, I didn't have far to go. Then again, I hadn't a clue where it was I was going to.

I valet parked my car and ran inside the hotel, my shirt buttoned up, my nipples pounding with each step. I was sure I'd ripped a hole in my briefs, my cock was so fucking stiff now. Midway into the lobby, however, I stopped. "X marks what spot?" I whispered to myself, my neck craning this way and that.

And then a smile lit up my face. "X," I practically shouted, with a snap of my fingers. "The Roman numeral for ten." I stared up and counted the floors. "Ten. Go figure."

I raced to the elevator, the lump in my slacks swinging to and fro. I pounded the button for the tenth floor, my breath ragged, foot impatiently tapping away as the metal cage crept up and up and up. Then, *ding*, I was there.

The halls were empty, stretching way down on both sides. I thought to holler his name, but figured that would be cheating. I looked from door to door. They went from 1001 to 1050. I thought of what number would have the most significance, the number that would mean the most to both of us. And then it hit me. We met on October tenth. 10/10.

"Worth a shot."

I ran down the hall, horny as a schoolboy, a spreading stain in my slacks from all the leaking my cock was doing. I knocked on the door, drumming out the song with my knuckle. "Skyrockets in flight," *tap*, *tap*, "afternoon delight." I waited. Nothing. Not a friggin' peep. Still, something told me he was just on the opposite side. Call it a pull. A connection.

I tried the door: locked. "Fuck. Now what?" I scratched my head and stared at the handle, the card slot without the card. I stood there, stock-still, my nipples in glorious agony, chaffing beneath the unrelenting clips.

And then that smile of mine reappeared.

"Put these on," the note in my car had read. "You'll need them later."

I looked around. I was still alone in the hall, so I opened my shirt, my fingers trembling as each button popped, the cold corridor causing goose bumps to run rampant down my arms. Gently, I unhinged the clamps, sighing as my nipples, at last, were set free. I dropped the device to the carpet, the light from beneath the door shining off the silver chain.

"Knock, knock," I rasped, crouching down and sliding one of the clips into the crack, the end disappearing under the door before the chain got pulled taut. I grinned. "Bingo." The chain went slack. I pulled it back through, the end now clamped on to a card key. I stood back up, cupping my rigid prick in the palm of my hand. "Time to go digging for treasure, sport."

My heart pounded as I slid the card down the groove, the door creaking open, the bed coming into view, his stupendous ass there to greet me.

"Took you long enough," he chided, face to the wall, legs wide apart; dick pushed down, throat-gagging thick.

I shut the door behind me. "Difficult to run with a perma-frozen erection, dude." I kicked off my loafers and slid down my slacks, drawn in like a moth to a flame. My briefs quickly followed suit, fat prick swaying before zeroing in on its target. My dress shirt hit the floor as my face dove in, tongue at the ready.

He moaned appreciatively as I lapped my way inside, a palm rising high before slamming down on his upturned rump, the sound echoing around the room as the motion was repeated. "Lunch," he offered.

I tugged on his balls, yanking them back, his dick following, plum-sized head dripping as I gave it a gentle smack. "You're lucky I'm a meat and potatoes kind of guy." My mouth traveled south, tongue gliding over hairy nuts before I sucked his dick in, all that flesh widening inside, filling every millimeter of space possible. My moan matched his groan, his dick now pumping down my throat, my index finger zooming around his hole before gliding in and up and back.

"Fuuuck," he exhaled.

I popped his prick out of my mouth. "I'm getting to that." Again I slapped his ass, a flush of red spreading through the alabaster, and then I hopped on the bed with him, flipping him over, legs wide, arms behind his head. "Howdy," I said.

"Good day at work?" he replied, with a wink.

I chuckled. "Getting better by the second." I bent over him, his sparkling blue eyes drawing me in like a pool on a hot summer's day. My lips brushed his, a spark jumping the gap that sizzled down the length of my back, his tongue jutting out to meet mine.

"Mmm," he hummed.

"Mmm," I echoed, our mouths colliding, meshed together, eyes open wide, not wanting to miss a second of the action.

His legs rose up and out, feet finding their way above my ass, locking me in, my dick instinctively pressed to his crack, gliding and sliding over his hole. I grabbed his hands and pinned them down on either side of his head, our noses Eskimo kissing as I teased my way inside of him, just the head, slow and easy, a gentle inch, then two. His eyelids briefly fluttered; he gave a sharp inhale, then a satisfied exhale.

"More," he pled, a perfect kiss on my lips.

"No problem," I replied, giving a shove forward, halfway inside now, his asshole sucking me in, tight as a drum.

Another kiss. Then another. "More."

I smiled, my hands locked with his. "Greedy fucker." And then the final shove inside, my dick slamming against his farthest reaches, the length and breadth of it buried inside, until my balls bounced off his cheeks. "Better?" I asked.

He nodded and rocked me with his feet, my cock pushing in, sliding out, in and out, slow and easy, waves of pleasure washing over me with each thrust, a sigh from him with each extraction. Again our lips met, more insistent this time, hungry, as my pace picked up. A steady glide all the way in. A steady glide all the way out. *Pop.* Then rapid successions of piston fucks, his breathing shallow now, a string of moans running rings around us.

"Let 'er rip," he grunted, writhing beneath me.

With my dick now in charge, I had little choice. Sweat pouring down my back, a pool of it between his pecs, my rod went into overdrive, fucking his hole for all it was worth, pounding it silly, slamming, slamming, slamming away; my cock and his ass on fire from all that awesome friction.

I pulled my hands from his and sat up on my knees, his

fist instantly around his prick, stroking hummingbird fast, his balls rising, his prostate as hard as granite. I whipped my dick out just as it shot, just as he shot, both our cocks exploding in a torrent of white-hot come, coating his belly in a sea of spunk as our moans reached their blissful crescendo, our bodies trembling and jerking, my knees buckling. Gasping for air, I collapsed on top of him, his arms around me as he fought to catch his breath.

"How long do you have the room for?" I whispered in his ear.

He laughed. "When do you need to be back at work?"

I hopped off the bed and retrieved my cell phone. "Cancel my afternoon, Beth."

She paused. "Something else come up, Rick?"

I stared down at my partner, the love of my life, his sweaty body twisted in the mess of sheets. "Come up?" I gazed down at my cock, a smile stretching wide across my face. "Let's just say you might want to look out the window in about an hour." I gave my dick a tug. "There's gonna be skyrockets."

She sighed. "In the middle of the afternoon, Rick?"

I laughed, my dick already starting its joyful rise. "Best time of the day for them, Beth," I told her, shutting off my phone. "Best time of the day for them."

BREAKFAST
IN BED

Hank Edwards

Morning sex is not for everyone. My partner and I have been together for a little more than eleven years now, and Sunday mornings have become a haven for us; a slow, sexy way to start the day and begin the week. We awake slowly, our nude bodies entwined beneath the sheet, arms around each other, lazy morning hard-ons pressing against thigh or buttock. After so many years of waking up with Ted, I can pretty much tell when things are about to go from idly investigative to seriously interested.

This morning is similar to most of the others we've shared. The sheer white curtains diffuse the early morning sunlight, the birds are conversing outside the window, and Ted rolls over to slide his arm across my chest, his fingers softly rubbing my nipple. I sigh and turn my head to kiss his grizzled cheek and he rises up to kiss my mouth, his tongue flicking quickly across my lips. On Sundays we deal with morning breath.

His hand moves up from my nipple to cup the back of my

shaved head. His strong fingers read the familiar curve of my skull and rest in their usual places among the bumps he refers to either as my knowledge bumps or evidence I was dropped on my head as a child, depending on how impressed or angry he is with me at the time. His palm guides my head, turning me to face him, and he slides closer, his leg draping over my hips so his thigh rubs against my erection. His kiss intensifies and a moment later our lips part. His tongue rolls into my mouth, always welcome, hot and skilled as it pushes against my own.

I moan quietly and he responds in kind. His cock, at full mast now, throbs against my hip. My hands slip around his body to move up and down his back, massaging the rugged terrain of his spine. Ted pulls his face back and I gaze into his sleepy blue eyes and smile.

"Morning," he says, voice thick and rough.

"Morning," I reply.

He kisses me again, the action slow, timeless, his tongue making circles in my mouth then backing away to invite mine to probe. We kiss for a long time, our hands roving over the bodies we know so well, finding the spots we know enjoy being touched, applying pressure to the areas most often knotted with tension.

Ted releases the back of my head and, still kissing me, moves his fingers down my chest, parting the hair and stopping to pinch my nipple. I groan in response and the pressure of his fingers increases. My cock thumps against his thigh and he begins to move his leg slowly up and down, rubbing my erection and spreading the precum bubbling up at the tip.

Ted pulls back and grins. "You've sprung a leak."

I smile up at him. "Guess you should plug me up."

He closes his eyes and leans in to kiss me a little longer before his lips move down to my chin, kissing and sucking at the weekend whiskers showing a little more gray than last year. His mouth slips down to my throat, sucking lightly, his tongue licking the sleep sweat from my skin. Down the middle of my chest he goes, running his tongue through the hair and over the skin. He is working both my nipples now, pinching them, twisting them, bringing them up into hard points of longing.

"Oh, god," I breathe and reach down to run my hands through the whirls and spirals of his sleep-tangled hair. "I love you."

Ted moves lower still, dipping his tongue into the well of my navel, his fingers still tweaking my nipples. He moves his chest back and forth across the length of my hard-on, smearing precum into his hair and skin.

He releases my nipples to push the sheet completely off us, kicking it away with his feet as he gets to his hands and knees above my hips. I raise my head to watch as he takes my cock in his hand, curling his fingers around the shaft and slowly pumping his fist along its length. He purses his lips around the slippery head and runs his tongue over the satin surface, licking up the precum his hand is squeezing out of me.

Ted parts his lips and takes me down his throat with practiced precision, swallowing me whole. I let out a deep groan and arch my back, plunge my hands into his hair as I thrust up into him. His lips press down into my bush, clamped tight around the base of my cock. His thumb finds the sweet spot just beneath my heavy, shaved balls and I groan again.

Ted backs off my cock until his lips grip the cap, where he sucks. His mouth makes hungry, slurping sounds as he bobs his head, his hand stroking the shaft in time with his motions. I groan and writhe beneath him, grabbing fistfuls of the bottom sheet as his mouth works its magic on me.

He knows when I am close and pulls his mouth off my dick,

his hand slowly squeezing and caressing, easing me back from the edge of orgasm. I catch my breath and look down to where he is smiling up at me.

"I love to drive you crazy," he says.

"You do it every day, and not always in bed," I reply and sit up, grabbing him and pushing him down onto his stomach. I lie atop him, stretched out along his back, my hard, spit-slick cock nestled between the furry mounds of his ass. I caress his shoulders and arms, massaging the muscles. Moving down, I run my hands along his spine, fingers digging into each group of muscles and pressing out the tiny knots from his workweek. He moans and sighs beneath me.

"God, Ray," Ted says, his voice muffled by the mattress. "I love Sunday mornings."

"Me too." I move lower still, straddling the backs of his thighs as I work on the small of his back, my fingers sifting through the patch of soft, downy hair. I slide my hands lower and focus my attention on the firm, hairy globes of his ass, kneading them, digging into the muscles and spreading them open now and again to glimpse the dark pink ring of his anus camouflaged beneath wispy brown hair. Ted clenches his sphincter, making it wink at me.

I spread his asscheeks wide and lean down to touch the tip of my tongue to his hole. Ted sighs and opens his legs wider. I press my lips against the wrinkled velvet muscle and slide my tongue into him. I lick and suck at his asshole, rimming him good and deep. My cock throbs as I work, dripping precum onto the sheet.

Ted gets to his knees, raising his hips and pressing his forehead into the mattress, groaning as my tongue burrows deep into him. I move back and slip a finger into the dark, glistening hole, probing the familiar warm depths. I slide my other hand down between his legs to rub his perineum then up to his shaved balls, tugging on them as I finger-fuck his ass.

"Oh, god," Ted gasps. "Get another finger up there."

My first finger is joined by a second and I resume fucking him, slowing now and then to bend the knuckles and reach into the well-mapped territory of his ass to stroke the hard nub of his prostate. Ted shudders and moans before me, raising his torso from the mattress only to collapse against it once again.

I finally ease my fingers from his dank depths and he turns, pulling me to the mattress, his strong arms pinning me down as he straddles my hips. His kiss is more urgent than when we started, his tongue forceful in my mouth, his lips pressing harder. He takes both our cocks in his fist and strokes them, faster and faster, until we each near the edge. Moments before it is too late to go back, he opens his grip and we both look down to watch as a small puddle of cum pumps out of his cock onto my balls. Ted can take himself right to the edge several times, letting out just a little cum, before he finally lets go and unleashes a gusher of a cum shot.

He scoops up the cum with his fingers and pushes my hips in the air, higher, higher, until I am nearly perpendicular to the mattress. My head is bent at an awkward angle and I am staring up at the glistening head of my own cock aimed directly down at my face. Precum dribbles off the end and I open my mouth to catch it on my tongue.

Ted holds me up with one palm against the small of my back: the other hand, the one that scooped his cum, is held up out of the way as he lowers his mouth to my anus. He licks and sucks at my furrowed sphincter, spearing his tongue into me then running it along the shaved surface of my perineum to suck on my balls.

Taking his mouth from my ass, Ted spreads his cum across

my anus and slips his spunk-smeared finger deep inside me a few times. Getting to his feet, Ted gets his balance on the tricky surface of the mattress then lifts a leg to plant one foot by my head, keeping the other behind me. He is straddling the open V of my legs, holding on to an ankle with one hand as with his other he aims his cock down at my cum-slick hole. The swollen, fleshy cockhead parts the lips of my anus and slides into me sideways, pushing a gasp out of my mouth.

Slowly Ted fills me with the full length and girth of his cock, pushing himself down into my asshole. The position is unusual; he has never done this to me before, and my body breaks out in a sweat as my insides adjust to this new path of invasion.

"Oh, fuck," I say. "Where'd you learn this?"

Ted smiles. "I've been thinking about this for a while. I think I saw it in one of those movies we bought off the Internet."

He stops when he is buried inside me, joined with me so intimately, and we look at each other for a moment. My left hand grips his ankle as I slowly stroke myself with my right. Ted tips his head, staring at the sight of my sphincter stretched taut around the fat column of his cock.

"That is so fucking hot," he says, rubbing my balls with his free hand.

And then he begins to really fuck me. He pushes down with his feet, bouncing on the mattress, pile driving into me. I can hear the slick, wet sucking sound of his cum-lubed cock each time it pulls out and plunges back into me. His dick pummels me, stretching the rectal muscles I clench around him like a fist.

"Oh, yeah," Ted grunts. "Grab my cock. That's it. Oh, fuck, your ass is so fucking hot."

"Oh, god," I gasp. "I'm coming."

I slow my strokes to focus on the magic spot just beneath the head of my cock and open my mouth. The first squirt of cum lands on my cheek, the second and subsequent shots hit different areas of my face and throat as I am bouncing too fast to be able to aim very well. Ted watches me cum on my own face then pulls my leg in close so he can run his tongue around my toes, sucking them and licking the bottom of my foot.

"Oh, fuck yeah," he says quietly and I can tell by the tone of his voice he's getting close. "Oh, god. Oh...oh, yeah!"

He pulls out of my ass and drops my legs, falling to his knees to straddle my chest, his thighs pinning my arms to my sides. He grabs his balls and jerks his cock, his fist a blur along the sturdy, glistening length of his shaft. When he sucks in a deep breath and raises his ass from my stomach I open my mouth.

His cum washes over my face and floods my mouth. I swallow it greedily, always hungry for the taste of his jizz. Ted's breathing slows as he squeezes the last of his cum up through the shaft and lets it drip into my open mouth. He uses the sticky, softening head of his cock to smear the stuff around my face then drops his dick into my mouth and I suck it clean.

Ted leans down to kiss me, his tongue darting quickly into my mouth. We get out of bed and I pad behind him into the bathroom where I begin to wash my face with a damp wash-cloth. Ted brushes his teeth then stands behind me, pulling my ass up against his soft cock.

"Want a donut from down the street?" he asks, flicking his tongue in my ear.

"Yeah, that would be good."

"What kind?" He steps to the door then turns back.

I give him a grin and use my tongue to clean some crusted cum from the corner of my mouth. "Why, glazed, of course."

SOMETHING DIFFERENT

Kyle Lukoff

The last thing he wanted was to remember.

As Johnny got dressed that night he chose clothing with the fewest associations attached to them. That leather vest he had picked up practically for free at the thrift store near his apartment. Those jeans were 501s, but he had bought them years before, just liking the way they were cut. Same with his boots—he had half a dozen pairs, Fryes and Wescos and Doc Martens, all associated with a particular fetish, but he picked a particularly scuffed pair that he had gotten before he knew what it meant to be a boot man.

The only real problem was his leather wristband. It had been his first present, and for five years it never left his arm. On his right wrist there had once been a strip of pale skin, untouched by the sun at Folsom Street Fair or Dore Alley or the outdoor patio at the Eagle.

Johnny picked it up off his dresser, rubbing the leather with a wistful sigh. How good it would feel on that wrist again, holding him tight. Telling the world that he wanted to give up control, wanted a man to take him in and provide the love and discipline he had craved his whole life.

But, no: he couldn't go there again, not so soon. He shook his head resolutely and, a little clumsily, snapped it onto his left wrist.

Johnny had felt like his life had truly begun the night he met Richard. He was thirty-five years old, freshly divorced and recently gay. He had left his wife in the desolation of Bakersfield and moved north to San Francisco, unconsciously living a tired old story that nonetheless felt new and exciting. He threw himself into "the lifestyle" with abandon. Circuit parties, glory holes, Sunday morning brunch: he loved it all.

He even became a regular at the Eagle, that notorious leather bar in the heart of SoMa. He picked up a few pieces of leather clothing, liking how butch it made him look. Johnny played around a bit, trying cock rings and clothespins and once a riding crop, but he never delved too deeply into that world.

Until he met Richard, that is.

It started out as a typical Sunday beer blast. Johnny was with some friends watching the crowd, and he happened to glance over toward the bootblack chair. The guy sitting in the chair looked hot, older with dark hair and a craggy face, so Johnny made eye contact and gave a half nod with a half smile on his face. The man looked at him sternly and turned his head away.

Johnny rolled his eyes. *Just another queen,* he thought, and turned back to his friends and the crowd.

Hours later, as he was getting ready to leave, he turned around after putting his beer bottle on the bar and almost bumped into someone. "Sorry, pal," he said, before looking up at the person's face. It was the man from the bootblack chair. Up close he was tall and imposing, and, acting on some instinct he didn't even recognize, Johnny crossed his arms behind his back.

"Good boy," said the man, and he grabbed Johnny by the collar of his leather shirt and shoved him into a dark corner.

They only left the corner to go to the man's apartment. Richard had a fully stocked playroom and Johnny had a seemingly endless well of energy, enthusiasm and excitement. By the time the scene ended Johnny knew he had found his calling.

With Richard's collar around his neck Johnny jumped into the leather community with both feet, turning up his nose at the drugging and dancing cliques he had only recently called home. He was Richard's boy, and at every conference, contest and fundraiser he could be found standing slightly behind his right shoulder. They played in public and private, and soon gained a reputation for being one of the more adventurous couples around. Johnny learned the ins and outs of floggings and needles and sounds, electro and single tails and water sports. Being with an Old Guard leatherman like Richard was a crash course in dominance and submission, and he soon learned to end every statement with "Sir," and to not capitalize his name in his presenter biographies. In submission, Johnny found his freedom.

He winced at the memories that flooded through him as he picked up his keys and had to stop himself from clipping them to the right side of his belt. With only a slight fumbling of the key chain he switched them to the left and stepped out of his apartment.

The relationship had ended badly. They were polyamorous, in theory, but Richard had found himself a new boy, younger, fresher, more malleable than Johnny. At first he had thought that Richard would keep the two of them as brothers, but he found himself slowly edged out of the relationship. Richard refused to end it formally. Johnny was still in love with him, but was unwilling to accept the crumbs of what had once been his meal. So he left, packed up his leather gear and took his name off the mailing lists, swearing he would never play again.

That was a year ago. Johnny had kept his head down and stayed out of the scene. He went to work. He came home and cleaned his apartment. Sometimes he'd go out with his room-mate to an art exhibit or a film screening, but he shied away from anything even remotely sexual. He dated a little, slept around a bit, but he found himself comparing everyone to the man he had lost and in turn found them wanting.

And yet he couldn't stay away, not completely. He found himself drawn to leather and BDSM-themed erotica. Solitary walks would involuntarily take him south of Market, and he would walk past the shops and the bars, daring himself to go in and never quite making it. He couldn't imagine leather without Richard.

But an ember still burned within the ashes of his heart. So that night, a year into his imposed solitude, he decided to go out again. A new play party had just started up in a venue he and Richard had never frequented. So Johnny got ready.

He couldn't bottom, of course. Not with someone else, not with all the feelings and thoughts and old hurts it would bring up. That night, he decided to go as someone else. That night he decided to top.

He was relieved that he didn't recognize the guy at the door, or the guy working coat check. After paying the entrance fee and taking off his shirt and jacket, Johnny took a look at the space. It was good sized, though not particularly well equipped. Johnny was used to wide-open playspaces with slings and St. Andrew's crosses and suspension bondage sites, but this space was different. It was labyrinthine, with numerous alleyways and secluded corners. One area had mats on the floor, and he saw what looked like two women wrestling, with a small group watching.

The more he looked around, the more pleased he became. Johnny was used to men-only parties. Richard was uncomfortable playing around women, and thought that dykes and straight people who did leather were corrupting the spirit of what had been a masculine way of life. Johnny had verbally agreed with his Master, but privately had thought the more the merrier. This party certainly seemed to take that stance. It was still early but there were already several couples playing, two straight couples and a threesome of women. However, the men who had taken his money and his clothes were decked out in leather and seemed gay, and Johnny hoped that more gay men showed up—while he was perfectly comfortable in mixed spaces, he wasn't personally interested in playing with women.

He set down his toy bag (not much in it: just a flogger, some condoms and lube and his favorite paddle) and stood against a wall where he could still see some action. Johnny also made sure to stay within sight of the door, so he could keep an eye on who showed up.

A steady stream of perverts came through the door, and Johnny didn't recognize any of them. There were a lot of women, some of whom looked like they might have once been men; a lot of cute, impossibly young-looking boys; a few couples that looked straight; a fair number of men, but most of them were of the creepster variety who stared open-mouthed at anything with cleavage.

Johnny began to shift uncomfortably. Was he going to be the only gay leatherman there? But just as he voiced that concern to himself, he saw him.

Like most of the boys at the party, this one appeared incredibly young and was too cute to believe. He was in boots, jeans and a leather vest, bare-chested with a scruffy little beard and a shaved head. He just screamed faggot, so Johnny kept an eye on him.

The boy seemed to know everyone. He floated from group to group doling out hugs and kisses, exchanging how-are-yous just out of Johnny's earshot. However, though he appeared to be friends with most people there, he didn't seem connected to any of them. When he was done greeting people he stood off to the side, at a loss, while others continued to flirt and negotiate. After a moment he took up a post against the same wall as Johnny and gazed out into the fray.

What should a Top do in this situation? Johnny asked himself. *Approach the boy? Wait to be approached?* Hell, he didn't even know if the kid was a bottom. As he stood there wrestling with himself he saw the boy turn toward him and look him up and down quickly. Then he turned his head back toward center and stared ahead, seemingly nonchalant but with a stiff neck.

Johnny took this as a good sign. He recognized the classic cruise and figured that if the kid wasn't interested he would move on. His determination not to make prolonged eye contact could be chalked up to shyness or good manners, so Johnny moved in.

"Hey there."

The kid flinched, startled. "Oh! Hi! I mean, um, hey, how's it going?"

Johnny smiled. What a cutie. "I like this space. You ever been here before?"

The boy shook his head. "Nope. I think it's new."

"Oh. Thought you might've been, you sure seem to know

everyone here. I'm John, by the way."

"I'm Corey. Yeah, I mean, it's a new space but the same old crowd. Never seen you before, though!"

"Nope, I don't know anyone here."

"You want me to introduce you to folks?"

John-neé-Johnny showed his teeth in what he hoped was a predatory grin. "No. I've seen all I want to."

It must have worked. The boy blushed and rubbed the back of his neck, but didn't move away. If anything, he seemed to lean in closer.

John lowered his voice to a gruff rumble. "So, boy, what are you into?"

Corey shrugged. John waited a moment, but that seemed to be all the answer he was going to get, so he prodded a bit.

"Does that mean anything goes? Flogging, fisting, fucking? You're down for whatever? Anywhere? Does that mean"—at this he grabbed the boy by his vest and pulled him close—"I could take you right here and do whatever I wanted?"

Corey whimpered but didn't struggle, and his eyes filled with longing.

"Sir, I—"

"What? You're allowed to have limits, boy. Just tell me what you want."

"All of that, Sir, I like all of it. But I'm, um, eff-tee-em."

"Eff-tee-em? What's that?" John was a bit puzzled. Was that some new term for poz or something?

"Uh, trans? Gender? It means I'm a boy, just with, um, different parts down below."

Something clicked in John's head. "Oh! FTM. Um. Okay. That's, uh, different. I've read about you guys. So what kind of surgeries have you had?"

Corey hesitated. "Sir, are you...are you still interested?

Because if you are we can talk about my body and what you can do to it, but if you're not...then it's—I mean, it's not really your business, right?"

John blinked. He wasn't quite sure what to do and wanted to stall for time.

"Stay right here, boy, I gotta take a leak. When I come back I'll tell you what I want to do to you."

"You're not just going to leave, are you?" There was a plaintive note in Corey's voice.

"No, boy, I'm not just going to leave." The idea had run through his head, but John didn't want to be a prick. "Just stay there, at attention, and I'll be right back."

Corey's arms snapped behind his back at perfect angles, and John nodded in satisfaction.

Once in the bathroom he locked the door behind him and looked himself in the eye. He was more than a little freaked out, to be honest. It had been years since he had left his wife, and he had plunged into a world of dicks, balls and assholes with abandon. While he never engaged in the pussy-bashing of his more misogynist compatriots, he unthinkingly accepted the superiority of cock to those other, more secretive parts.

On the other hand...he had come to the party, in part, to learn something different about himself. In a split second he made up his mind. This could be a very good opportunity, indeed.

He washed his hands and went back out to the party. Corey was still standing where he had been left, arms behind his back, looking straight ahead. His face was impassive, but John could see that behind his back the boy was wringing his hands.

John walked up to the boy unhesitatingly and grabbed him by the belt buckle. "Come with me." With Corey dragged along behind, Johnny found an unoccupied padded bench, partitioned off by black plywood walls with holes cut into the sides for the voyeuristic. John shoved the boy onto the bench on his belly and straddled him.

Bending over John started whispering into Corey's ear.

"So now that I've got you here, boy, what do you want?"

"You're okay with...with me, Sir? My—"

"You wouldn't be here if I wasn't. Now tell me what you want. That's an order."

"I want...I want you to fuck me, Sir. And I want a spanking."

"Good boy. I had an eye on your ass the second you walked in. Now take off your pants."

John got off the bench and watched the boy strip down to a pair of tight green briefs. He went to lie back down but John stopped him.

"All the way, boy."

Corey bit his lip. "Are you sure, Sir?"

"You don't want me to have to tell you again."

With that implied threat Corey slowly took off his underwear. He did in fact have an adorable butt, lightly furred and cutely rounded, small but not flat. His front was a thick thatch of pubic hair, underneath which John could make out his finely shaped nether regions. Before he could get a closer look the boy lay down on his belly again.

John stood over him and started rubbing his ass and his back. When the flesh was warm and responsive to the touch he slapped the boy's left buttcheek, and then the right, lightly, to see how he would react. Corey breathed a bit heavily and stuck out his ass, inviting more.

John remembered how it felt to get a good spanking, and he was confident in his abilities to deliver one. He started striking lightly and evenly on both cheeks until the flesh was nice and red. Corey's breathing grew heavier with each blow, and then

John really started laying into him with stinging slaps, focusing first on one cheek, then the other.

Just as Corey seemed to be blissing out on the sensation John stopped. Corey looked up to see him taking off his belt and doubling it up in his right hand. After gently rubbing away some of the ache with his left hand he began whaling on the boy with it, hitting him solidly and hard, leaving dark red welts neatly lined up one next to the other. Corey became more vocal, crying out loudly. At one point the word "Stop!" flew out of his mouth.

With that John dropped the belt and grabbed a glove from the nearby safer-sex table. He snapped it on and rubbed Corey's ass again, hard but soothingly, pressing down on the sore spots but not making any new ones. Slowly he worked his way into the crack, pressing up against the boy's asshole, then dropping his hand a bit farther to rub against his front hole.

Corey started to whimper.

"That feels good, boy?"

"Yes, yes, Sir."

"Which hole do you want to get fucked in?"

"I...I like them both, Sir."

"Good."

Remembering safer-sex 101 John decided to focus on his butt first, then move to the front using a different glove. Putting that plan into action he began playing with Corey's asshole, exploring how many fingers he could get inside, how deep, how wide. Soon Corey was moaning loudly with pleasure, just saying, "Yes, Sir, please, Sir," over and over again. John grinned as he noticed many different pairs of eyes peeping in through the various viewing holes and the entrance way—apparently Corey's many friends knew he was getting some action and wanted to get in on it. If anything the audience just made John bolder, more determined to prove his topping ability to himself and others.

With a jolt John came back to his own body and realized that his dick was rock hard. He withdrew his hand slowly from the boy's asshole and grinned as Corey shuddered with pleasure.

He waited for Corey to crane his neck around and look him in the eye. His face was shiny with sweat, his eyes inquisitive.

"I'm sorry, Sir, am I being too loud?"

"Not at all, boy. I'm just thinking about what I want to do to you next."

"Next?"

"Yes. I'm not finished with you yet. Sit up."

The boy complied.

John stepped up so that his crotch was at Corey's eye level. "Unbutton my pants and get to work."

Corey slipped off the bench and got to his knees. He untucked John's dick from his pants and started sucking. While enthusiastic, it wasn't the most skillful blow job John had ever received—the boy seemed to have trouble taking Johnny's only moderate length.

"Wrap your hand around my dick, boy, and jerk me off while you suck me." After Corey had followed those directions the blow job improved mightily, so John put his hands around the boy's head, leaned back and enjoyed it.

After a few minutes of that, John tapped the boy on the shoulder and told him to get back on the bench, this time on his back. While he positioned himself Johnny slipped on a condom.

This time John joined Corey on the bench. "Legs in the air, boy."

John took a little bit of time to acquaint himself with the boy's parts. He had what looked like a little dick, no doubt enlarged by hormones. Below that was an opening, shaped differently from an asshole but not altogether foreign, flanked by two sets of lips, small inner ones and thicker outer ones. Looking at the boy John found that he wasn't reminded of his ex-wife at all. Nor was he reminded of his many nontransgendered male tricks. Corey's parts were just...different, which was what John had been looking for in the first place.

John leaned forward and sank into the boy's tight hole. He groaned deeply, surprised at how good it felt. Corey matched him loudly, and they fell into a rhythm together. Corey lifted his legs up higher to give John easier access, and soon John was pounding away with abandon. No matter how deep he went Corey's legs tightened around his back, urging him in more, harder, deeper.

At one point John looked down, wanting to watch his dick slam in and out, and was amazed at how hot it was. Not like fucking a woman, not the same as fucking an asshole accompanied by a cock and a pair of balls, but no less arousing. He let his eyes travel up the length of the boy's body, his round belly and hairy chest and sharply angled face, eyes rolled back into his head with pleasure.

Suddenly those eyes focused to meet John's, and under the intensity of the boy's stare John felt himself come closer to orgasm. He pumped in and out a few more times, grunting loudly and flooding the condom. He pulled out and smiled, mirroring the look on Corey's face.

The boy slowly sat up, using his hands for support. He was breathing heavily.

"Thank you, Sir."

"Thank you, boy. That was fun."

They stayed there awkwardly for a moment until Corey lunged forward and hugged John tightly. He mumbled something into his chest.

"What was that?"

Corey pulled back slightly. "That was my first time."

Johnny blinked in shock. "You mean you were a virgin?"

Corey laughed hard. "No! Definitely not a virgin. Just, that was my first time getting fucked by someone built like you."

"Oh. So you usually sleep with women?"

"Nah, other trans guys, mostly. I'm a fag, it's just hard to find dudes who are...you know, okay with my business."

"I am more than okay with your 'business,' boy. Just took a little getting used to."

With that they left the space. Their audience had tactfully dispersed, but once back in the common area Johnny caught Corey making eye contact with various people and grinning widely.

After a companionable silence Corey turned to John.

"So, I'm guessing you had a good time too?"

"More than a good time. And I'll tell you something, tonight was a first for me, too."

"First time with a tranny, you mean?"

"Well, yes, but also my first time topping."

Corey's jaw dropped. "You're joking."

John grinned proudly. "Not at all. I was a collared boy for years; never been called 'Sir' in my life."

"That's hilarious. First time for everything and, I guess, every*one*, right?"

"I guess so."

"Well"—Corey leaned against John's chest—"you ever want to practice again, I'll give you my number."

As it turned out, John wanted a lot more practice.

DRESSED TO IMPRESS

Heidi Champa

'm not wearing any underwear."

I looked up, trying not to choke on the sip of latte that had just passed my lips. A coughing fit soon followed and I tried to regain my composure as all eyes in the café started to turn my way. Blinking away stray tears, I finally found my voice.

"What did you say?"

"I'm not wearing any underwear. I seem to have forgotten to put them on this morning. I just thought I would mention it."

His eyes were shining; the corners of his mouth turned up in barely contained glee. His cup hit the saucer with a loud clank, and I watched as he shifted in his metal chair, clearly enjoying his freewheeling status.

"You forgot? How do you forget your underwear?"

"I don't know. I guess it just slipped my mind. I was in a hurry to meet you and I just slid on my pants without thinking."

"And you thought I should know?"

"Absolutely."

"Okay, well that's good to know."

"Don't you have anything to say about it?"

"What would you like me to say?"

He dropped his sports section, clearly feigning anger. His eyes were doing a lousy job of hiding his internal laughter, but his voice remained hard.

"So, what? It's not sexy when I don't wear underwear? Forgive me for trying."

I shook my head, trying to understand the bizarre situation I found myself in.

"Well, I'm just saying that traditionally, it's women who don't wear panties when they want to shake up a relationship. Not guys."

This time he laughed out loud. Now the curious eyes of the other patrons were on him, watching him cackle and struggle to regain his breath. I looked around, feeling self-conscious as he finally got quiet again.

"Traditionally? You're telling me there is a traditional way to shake things up? That might be the stupidest thing I've ever heard. God, Ben. Since when are you worried about tradition, especially when it comes to sex?"

He had me there. Lord knows, when we bought the leather restraints two months ago, tradition wasn't the first thing on my mind. However, this was different. Wasn't it?

"Look, Colin, don't take this the wrong way, but I'm just not that turned on by the thought of you naked under your khakis. Sorry. Free-balling doesn't really do it for me."

He sat back in his chair, and I waited for the comeback line that would put me in my place. It didn't come. He just picked up his sports page and his cup of black coffee and pretended I didn't exist. I couldn't truly believe that I had actually offended him, but he seemed really mad. After an eternity of tense minutes, our cups were empty. He stood without a word and took them to the plastic bin by the trash can, making a special effort not to look at me as he went. When he returned, I decided to deal with the problem directly.

"Come on, Colin. Don't be like this. It's not really a big deal, is it?"

"Just forget I said anything. Come on, we should go."

He stood quickly, turning toward the door before I could say anything else. I shook my head at his stubborn silliness, but at the same time, I couldn't help but stare at his ass as he walked. My mind was envisioning the naked flesh just below the thin material of his cargo pants before my rational mind could stop it. Despite my earlier declaration to the contrary, my body seemed to be reacting without my consent, blood flowing urgently to my cock. There was no way I was going to tell Colin that, though.

We carried on with our day, both pretending that everything was just fine. Colin finally started joking and behaving like his normal self, but I could tell he was still bothered by my dismissal of his attempts to be clever and cute. While he tried to make peace, I was trying to control the growing fire in my boxers as I watched his every move.

At the museum, while Colin looked at the walls lined with paintings, sculpture and photographs, I clocked the easy motion of his gait, my eyes focused between his legs and the naked cock that I now knew was under there. If he was uncomfortable at all, he didn't show it. As he climbed the stairs right in front of me, my eyes were back on his ass, watching the curve of his muscles play underneath his ratty old pants. My temperature was rising with each passing step and it had nothing to do with my lack of physical fitness. He turned and looked at me once he reached the top of the stairs, catching me in the act of gawking at his backside.

I cursed myself for having been so mean to Colin. Here I was, growing harder and hornier by the minute, and I had told him how stupid I thought he was for trying something new. He had put up with me and all my myriad sexual requests. He lived through the poison ivy he got when we fucked in the woods without a blanket and the chocolate and whipped cream stains that never came out of our brand-new sheets. All he did was try to make me smile while trying to make me hot, and I dismissed him.

We left the museum and I tried to think of a way to back-pedal on my previous slam of his free-balling ways, without losing too much face. So far, I had nothing.

As we sat in the darkness of the movie theater, I couldn't focus on the film. Every time he crossed his legs or moved in his seat, I found myself thinking about his naked dick brushing against the front of his pants, the contact his skin was making on the soft, just-washed material. It got so bad that I was blatantly staring at his crotch when a giant explosion made the entire crowd jump out of their chairs. I stayed stock still, too distracted to respond properly to an entire fictional town being demolished.

"Ben, what the hell are you doing? You're missing the best part."

His whispers startled me out of my trance, and I looked at his eyes in the dark. He turned back to the screen, just in time for more carnage to wow the audience. Instead of rejoining the story already in progress, I reached my hand out and put it right on his cock. Colin snapped his head over to look at me, his expression both confused and angry.

"What are you doing? Just watch the movie."

"I don't want to."

"Well, I do."

I didn't move my hand; in fact, I tugged at the obstinate zipper and worked my hand inside until I could feel the hot contact of his skin. Hidden as we were in the back row, I didn't worry about anyone seeing us, but I wasn't expecting him to grab my wrist in protest. He stopped short of pulling my hand away, but his grip wasn't allowing me to go any farther. My fingers strained to find the sensitive head of his cock, and as I ran the pad of my thumb over the slit, he released my wrist from captivity. His eyes stayed focused straight ahead, as I wrapped my fist around his now stiff prick. I watched his mouth fall open, just a little. At that moment, he could have yelled and no one in the theater would have heard him, the gunfire was far too loud. I jerked him gently at first, but couldn't contain my ardor as I felt him grow harder in response.

Colin surprised me by snaking his own hand under my shirt and tweaking my nipple, sending a warm jolt to my rock-hard cock. He smiled, knowing that my current aroused state wasn't just from his hard-on.

"So, I guess it turns out you were into the whole no-under-wear thing."

I couldn't answer as his thick middle finger met his thumb and pinched me hard, my nipple now as hard as my dick. The pain and pleasure was making my breath catch; the car chase on screen was doing a fantastic job of distracting the people around us from my moans. My fist squeezed him tight, my hand moving quicker as I felt my arousal barreling toward me as quickly as the runaway truck in the film. As suddenly as the crash scene disappeared, so did Colin's hand from my chest. My own hand disengaged as he sat up and zipped up in a hurry. Grabbing me by the arm, he led me through the lobby and into the deserted men's room. Once we were locked into the last stall, he looked down at me with a wicked smile.

"Admit it. Thinking about me without underwear turned you on after all. I mean, I know you like my dick, but there's no way just touching me made you that excited."

I hesitated, not wanting to give in to his requests, but I knew I was caught. He pinned my arms to the wall and just waited for my words to come.

"Yes. I admit it. I liked it. You've been driving me crazy all day."

He leaned down, acting as if he was going to kiss me, but he stopped short of my lips.

"You owe me an apology, I think."

"I know I do, Colin. I'm sorry for being such a pain earlier."

His smile made his lips graze mine and I pushed forward trying to make him kiss me.

"I need more than that."

He dropped his hands from mine, but I left them right where they were against the wall. I followed his movement with my eyes, until his hands were pulling my pants off. In the silence, I heard seams tearing as he yanked my boxers down and tore them from around my feet. Tossing them aside casually, he turned me around and bent me over, pressing my hands flat against the metal wall. I heard his zipper's metallic teeth opening as I stared at the graffiti-covered stall in front of me. My shirt moved up my back and his hands ran over my asscheeks slowly and deliberately. I expected a slap or two, but none came. Instead, the nudging head of his sheathed cock pushed at my ass. I felt a few gobs of spit land on my pucker, and his cockhead started to work inside me, barely teasing. I tried to keep quiet as he lubed me with his spit, taking his time inching inside me. I couldn't stand it, so I pushed back against him, taking him all the way inside me.

"Say it again, Ben."

"I'm sorry, Colin. I'm so sorry."

As I rambled out my apology, his cock repeatedly slammed into me, his hands on my hips controlling us both. I didn't have time to worry about someone finding us out; all I could think about was the quivering that was starting in my thighs as I rocked back and forth on my heels, taking Colin's cock to the hilt. My fingers curled into fists on the wall, my eyes closing to block out the fluorescent lights above us. I focused instead on the stars bursting behind my lids, the colors exploding as I pressed my eyes shut harder.

When I felt the familiar play of his fingers on my cock, I couldn't control myself anymore. Forcing myself back against his cock with abandon, I started to come, spurting against the wall in front of me. His jerking became faster as fresh flutters and shocks moved all through me, a last burst of come landing near my feet. My hands slid down the wall, as I couldn't keep them in place any longer. Just as I felt like I would hit the ground, Colin held me up as he came inside me, jolting us both forward as he groaned and shuddered against my back. I don't know where we found the strength, but we managed to stay off the floor, clutching each other as we regained some semblance of composure.

We straightened out, and I stared at my tattered underwear lying on the floor of the stall. Deciding to leave them behind, I smiled to myself as I pulled my pants up over my naked ass. Colin turned back to me, kissing me hard on the mouth before we left the bathroom, not worried about anyone seeing us coming out together.

We walked toward home, both of us still shaky. The night air went right through my shirt and gave me a chill, my shivers making Colin throw his arm around my shoulder.

"You know, Colin. I'm not wearing any underwear."

He laughed, his chest vibrating against my side as we crossed the street before an oncoming car could get any closer. I looked up at him and caught his smile before he put on a serious and pinched face.

"Sorry, Ben, but I'm just not that turned on by the thought of you naked under those jeans."

I knew I deserved that, but I jabbed him in the ribs anyway.

PUBLIC DISPLAYS OF AFFECTION

Logan Zachary

Quentin, we have a problem."

"Casey, you know I hate when you say that." Quentin walked down the long marble halls of the Minneapolis Institute of Art, the MIA.

"I'm down at the new display, and you're really going to hate what I've found," Casey said into his cell phone.

"What? The jockstraps on display?"

"The history of the uniform is far from jockstraps on parade, but I think we ordered the mannequins from the wrong place."

Quentin ran up the marble staircase to the second floor, heading in his direction. "Why? What's wrong? Did we get women? Children?"

"Worse." Casey said, as he inserted the arm into the mannequin and stepped back.

"We're gay men, and I know all we wanted were men. What did we get? Dogs and cats?"

"You'll have to see it to believe it," Casey said, then laughed.

Quentin passed the information desk and slipped under the rope with the sign, INSTALLATION IN PROGRESS. "I'm almost to the display area. Which room are you in?"

"I'm in the locker room."

"Ooo, my favorite one."

"Mine too."

As Quentin walked into the locker room display, a naked man's backside greeted him: a perfect bubble butt. His skin was tan and beautiful. "Casey, why are you naked?"

Casey's head popped up over the naked man's shoulder. "I'm not, but I'm admiring the artwork."

Quentin did a double take and noticed a seam above the man's ass and one by each shoulder. "That's the mannequin? Wow! They're so realistic."

"You ain't seen nothing yet." Casey swiveled the male model around.

An enormous penis hung between his legs, thick and veined with a thick bush of dark pubic hair. A mass of fur covered each pec and thinned as it lowered across washboard abs.

"Impressive," Quentin said. "He's almost as big as you are."

"Thanks for the compliment, but I think you're missing something."

"Doesn't look like he's missing anything at all."

"Exactly."

"What? Oh. OH! Now I see. Are they all like that?"

Casey nodded his head. "Oh, yeah. Some even better than him."

"The exhibit opens in two days." Quentin ran his hand over the chest of the mannequin. His fingers combed through real hair and the skin felt warm and realistic to the touch. He pulled his hand away as if burned.

"I know. It's creepy. It's almost like that movie *House of Wax*."

"What are we going to do?"

"I've called Sportin' Men, and they don't have any other models in stock."

"We've always ordered from Sporting Men before; they're great."

"I know, but these are from Sportin' Men." He stressed the *'n.'* "There is no *G,* and that's how they keep the two separate."

"I don't understand." Quentin walked around the man and felt his cock swell in his pants.

"Sporting Men have athletic bodies, Sportin' Men are anatomically correct and they're all sportin' wood, or some form of arousal."

"There are some fully erect?"

"Oh, yeah."

"Wonderful," Quentin said, sarcastically. "I've been sportin' wood since I walked in here." He lowered his hand to hide his arousal.

"I can see it from here, dear. Nothing I haven't seen before." Casey walked over to Quentin and kissed him.

Quentin gave him a quick peck and stepped back. "No PDA's—you know, public displays of affection at work."

Casey pointed down at Quentin's groin. "Tell your big buddy that."

Quentin looked around the locker room, wishing the showers really worked to take a cool shower.

Casey picked up a towel and wrapped it around the manne-quin's waist. "He's shy."

"Quentin, Mr. Rothenberg called to confirm his meeting with you tomorrow afternoon. He said he should arrive about one.

Did you want me to contact you as soon as he arrives or should I show him around, and then let you know?" Roberta Schwartz asked behind her desk.

Quentin rushed into his office, followed closely by Casey.

"Call me as soon as he arrives, and I'll meet him on the tour."

"Okay. Hi, Casey. How are you doing?"

Casey rolled his eyes and smiled. "We're trying to put out a possible fire in the new uniforms display."

Roberta looked shocked.

"Oh, no. Not a literal fire, just a small problem arose; I mean, came up." His face burned red.

"Stop making jokes at a time like this. Rothenberg is a huge contributor to the MIA. The last thing we need is a sex scandal to happen when he arrives. He hasn't written his check to us this year. He wants to inspect the new display and make sure it's worth his money."

"I'd pay to see it," Casey said, "and I get in free."

"You're not helping."

"I wanted to open the crates last week when they arrived, but someone wouldn't let me inspect them."

"So this is my fault?" Quentin said.

"I'm not blamin' no one."

Quentin flopped down into his chair and pulled out a folder on his desk. He flipped through a few invoices and found one. He picked up the phone and dialed.

"Could I speak to someone in the service department?"

Casey watched as he nodded his head.

"They've all left for the day?"

"I told you..." he started, but Quentin held up his hand, stopping him.

"Will anyone be in tomorrow? I see." He hung up the phone. "Shit."

"I told you," Casey said.

Quentin grabbed his arm. "Come on. We'll see what we can do."

Roberta watched as the two stormed out of the office. "Lovers shouldn't work in the same place." She returned to the report she was working on.

"What are we going to do?" Quentin walked over to an open crate and saw a ten-inch cock sticking straight up. It was thick and uncut, and a foreskin hung off the tip. His hand involuntarily reached forward and retracted the skin. A dark pink mushroom tip slipped out of the sheath. "Are these for medical students?"

Casey pulled a sheet of paper out of another crate and started to read it. "No. You're going to laugh when you hear this."

"I doubt that." Quentin continued to stroke the cock and worked his way down the shaft to the balls. The balls swung free as the fine hair tickled his fingers.

"They're used with sex workers for therapy."

"What?" Quentin's finger trailed underneath the testicles, which swung out of the way, and slipped along the crease. His finger found the anus. He circled the spot and felt it give under his pressure. He probed harder, and his fingertip inserted itself into a smooth canal. Pushing deeper, his whole finger entered. "Now I see," he said.

Casey stepped next to him and saw what he was doing. "Did you ask for permission?"

Quentin pulled out his finger and waved it at Casey. "Do I need to ask for permission?" He approached Casey; his finger still extended and grabbed him. He waved the finger under his nose.

Casey pulled his head back and laughed. "You're naughty."

Quentin hugged him close and said, "Well, should we get started?"

"Doing what?"

"Let's put them together and see what we have to work with. We'll try and dress them in the uniforms that fit and see if we can somehow tone down their assets."

Casey's hand caressed the front of Quentin's pants. "You're hard."

"Are you?" His hand explored Casey's inseam and found the same aroused flesh. "I think we need to get to work, before we get sidetracked."

Casey broke the embrace and started to assemble the man in the crate by them. This man was a leather bear if he ever saw one: thick furry chest and muscular hairy legs. His huge uncut cock stood out proudly. "I wonder if we could mold them into any position we want."

"That will help, but can we pad the uniforms?"

"They aren't big enough?"

"Yes," Quentin said. "I wanted to pad their shorts to cover up the bulge."

"These men are hung."

"Well, get tucking."

"I love when you talk dirty to me."

"Tuck you."

All the men were assembled and stood in the shower room. "I've died and gone to heaven," Casey said.

"I hope this is what heaven is like." Quentin looked at the bear. "So, what do you see him as? The football player?"

"That's what I was thinking." Casey picked up the duffle bag with the word FOOTBALL printed on the side. He unzipped the bag and pulled out the uniform. "Do we need the shoulder pads?" he asked as he dropped them on the floor. "His body looks big enough without them."

Quentin picked up the jock and stretched it out. "Do you think this will hide that?"

Casey laughed. "No."

"Could we cut it off?" Quentin asked, holding the man's cock.

"You can't. That's just wrong."

"Let's see if this works." Quentin picked up the mannequin and waited as Casey slipped the jock over his feet. His fingers slid between his buttcheeks and entered his hole. Quentin's erection sprang to full length in his shorts.

Casey pulled the white elastic up the hairy legs as Quentin set him down. He pulled the pouch over his dick and straightened his butt straps. The mesh stretched to its limit.

"Huge," was all Quentin said. They slipped on the white football pants and inserted the pads. Casey tied the laces at the waistband. The pants tented in front of the man, but it looked like it would work.

"Do we have to put his shirt on?" Casey asked. "I've always had a football fantasy."

"You want to be the tight end?"

"I already am." He slapped his butt. Casey pulled out a Speedo and dangled it from his finger. "Who gets to wear this?"

Quentin searched for a swimmer's body and found a perfect one. He picked him up, as Casey looped the leg holes over its feet. As Quentin set him down, Casey worked the Speedo into place.

"There isn't enough material."

"Leave it, what a great fantasy and look."

* * *

For the next few hours, Quentin and Casey dressed each mannequin with the perfect uniform, deciding who would get the chain mail, and which one looked like a hockey player, a runner or a knight, and which mannequin would play cricket, basketball or soccer.

Quentin's phone rang, but he ignored it. They were having too much fun playing dress up.

Finally, all but one mannequin was dressed.

"So what should we do with him?" Quentin asked. He took the man into his arms and danced around the other men.

Casey took Speedo man and joined in the dance. "Trying to make me jealous?"

Quentin caressed the mannequin's body; he cupped his buttocks and dug into his bubble butt. His finger explored the opening. "How do you suppose the sex workers use these?"

Casey spun around and slipped his hand into the blue Speedo. "I would guess that they use them to try all the things they are afraid to try with another person."

"Do you think these openings are usable?"

"Only one way to find out." He set Mr. Speedo down and took Quentin's partner. "You always enjoyed a bubble butt, and this one is perfect."

"I wouldn't say that. Your ass is perfection." Quentin kissed Casey.

"PDA at work. PDA anywhere. What gives?" Casey started to unbutton Quentin's shirt. He rubbed his hands over the thick mat of hair that covered his chest. He pinched his nipples and felt them rise up into points under his touch.

"I've been hard since we started this."

"Me too."

Casey's hands unbuckled Quentin's belt and unzipped his fly.

He reached in to pull out his uncut cock.

Quentin's erection sprang free of his pants.

Casey caressed down the shaft and felt precum ooze from the tip. It slid along his palm as Quentin threw his head back and moaned. His hands found Casey's T-shirt and pulled it over his head.

"You always wanted a threeway," Quentin said. "This could be our first."

"Fooling around at work is a first too."

"Stop talking," Quentin's mouth descended on Casey's and quieted him. His tongue explored and tasted his lover, as his hands undid Casey's jeans.

He kicked off his shoes and let his jeans slide to the floor. His Calvins clung to his body like a second skin. A wet spot formed at the tip of his dick in the sheer cotton. The outline of his mushroom head showed through the fabric. A dark shadow of pubic hair contrasted with the pale skin below.

Casey looked around and saw all the men staring at him in his underwear. He covered himself as he felt his arousal start to shrink.

"What's wrong?" Quentin asked.

"I've never been the center of attention before."

"It's kind of creepy, but it's also kind of hot and sexy." Quentin slipped his pants and underwear off. His erection bounced up and down with each beat of his heart. His foreskin was wet and a small drop of precum clung to the flap.

Casey licked his lips, but didn't move.

Quentin knelt down and pulled Casey's briefs off. He leaned forward and ran his tongue around the tip of his cock and kissed it. His lips puckered and drew Casey's semi-hard-on into his mouth.

Casey threw his head back as the warm wetness took him

and sucked his shaft. His erection stretched to a maximum length. Quentin grabbed his low-hanging balls and rolled them between his fingers.

Casey moaned in pleasure. His hand reached over to Mr. Speedo and rubbed his bulge. His fingers pulled the fabric down and removed the cock from its restraint. He milked it as Quentin milked his dick with his mouth.

Quentin freed Casey's cock and said, "Don't come too fast, I have plans for you."

"Anything," Casey exhaled, as a shudder washed over his body. He almost pulled Mr. Speedo off of his feet.

A footfall echoed down the hallway display, but neither man cared.

Quentin worked Casey's arousal and felt his balls start to rise. "Take his Speedo off," he commanded.

"Why?"

"I want him to join in. I want to rim his ass and lube up his tight hole." Quentin wagged his tongue at Casey and smiled. "You're the one who wanted to try a threesome. This is perfect and no guilt."

Casey pulled the Speedo off, bent the mannequin over and held his cheeks open for Quentin.

Quentin's cock dripped with precum, lubing the opening. He pulled back his foreskin, allowing more clear fluid to escape. He painted it on the opening and pressed forward. The hole was tight and his girth was massive. He knelt and stuck his tongue between the fleshy orbs. He tasted his own juices and added saliva to the opening.

Casey knew what the mannequin was feeling, if rubber and plastic could feel. He twisted the model's head back and slid his cock into its mouth. The fleshy lips and tight tunnel formed suction on his engorged dick.

"You always wanted a spit roast." Quentin stood and drove his cock deep into the mannequin. His hips drilled his erection in deeper. The narrow passageway was also airtight and formed a vacuum around his dick.

The men slid the doll back and forth on their cocks. The pressure that drew down on them grew, adding to their pleasure and sensation.

"I'm going to come," Quentin said, as he grabbed the man's hips and slammed back into him.

Casey pulled on his ears and increased his speed. "Me... me...too."

Quentin drove into him one more time as his balls slammed into the bubble butt. They released their load and it shot out of his cock and filled the tunnel.

Casey's dick rolled across the mannequin's tongue and that extra wave was all it took. Cum burst out as he pulled back; the suction increased and pulled more out of his balls. He pushed in one more time and pulled back. A wet pop echoed in the room as his cock escaped from the lips.

The model snapped in half, as each man took his piece with him to the floor. Their fleshy asses hit the tile and both sweaty men clung to their half as if it were a life jacket.

Quentin withdrew from the perfect ass and lay back waiting for his breathing to return to normal. "Wow. That was hot."

"Yeah," was all Casey said.

Quentin crawled over to Casey and pulled him close. He kissed him deeply and whispered in his ear, "Do you know what I want?"

"Like that wasn't enough?" Casey laughed.

"I want to see him fuck you, fill you up."

"What?"

"I want to use his dick in your ass." Quentin turned his half of Mr. Speedo and stroked his cock. "Look how long and thick it is. You and I have never had anyone like that before...."

"And you think that will fit in me?"

"I would love to try." Quentin kissed him again.

"What's all of this? One of your fantasies you want to live out?"

Quentin's face reddened and he nodded. "Yes, is that so bad?"

"No," Casey agreed.

"We know he's clean and safe and won't tell anyone."

"He's the perfect man."

"No, you are."

"If I do this, right, I get..."

Quentin cut him off. "No, you are the prefect man for me, but this is something else."

Casey sat up and stared at the enormous cock. "I did feel sorry for the Speedo."

"Let's lube him up and see how it goes." Quentin milked his cock for what was left of his load and smeared it down the mannequin's shaft.

Casey pulled out a small bottle of lube. "Don't ask, but it's not for men, it's for some of the tight spots these pieces of art need to be slipped into."

Quentin nodded and took the bottle. "Let me apply it to you." He poured some on his hand and worked it around his fingers. "Bend over, baby."

Casey didn't look sure, but slowly he turned his butt to him.

"Beautiful." Quentin's hand slipped between the cheeks and greased his crease. His fingers ran over his opening, but teased it as they passed back and forth over it.

Casey moaned. "Do it, please." He widened his legs to allow easier access.

Quentin slipped his index finger to the hole, circled it and then probed.

"Deeper."

His finger pressed down harder.

"Deeper."

His finger slipped in to the first joint.

Casey rocked back on his knees and forced his ass onto Quentin's finger. It slipped in all the way to the knuckles. "Yesss."

Quentin tapped Casey's prostate and watched as his body rocked back and forth. Low animal moans escaped from him. Quentin used his other hand to stroke Casey's cock, which grew hard instantly.

"You're going to make me come again," he said.

"Is that a bad thing?" Quentin asked.

"No."

Quentin withdrew from Casey's butt and moved Speedo man's lower half into position. "Sit on him."

Casey moved over the erection and paused. "I need the upper half too. This way is too strange."

Quentin added the top half and secured it into place. "Ready?" Casey lowered his bottom, as Quentin aimed the mannequin's cock to the tender spot. Slowly, Casey descended on the ten inches. He felt the firm tip seek entry and he pressed down.

Quentin firmly grasped the mannequin's cock as he stroked Casey's buttcheek. "Relax," he soothed.

"With ten inches trying to rip me open?"

"Breathe out."

Casey exhaled and his sphincter relaxed. He felt the cock slide in. The mushroom head stopped where the girth prevented further entrance, but he sat down harder and stretched his muscle around and over it. Once in, the rest was thinner and glided deeper inside him.

"Good job," Quentin said.

Casey grasped the mannequin's shoulders and rode up and down on his cock. He threw his head back as he slid down the pole. Its pubic hair tickled his cheeks as pure bliss entered.

Quentin's erection returned and so did his desire to join in. "Get onto your hands and knees."

"Doggy style?"

"Please."

"Why?" Casey's rhythm increased and he didn't want to switch positions.

"Mannequin in the middle."

"You want to tap his ass?"

"Oh, yes."

Casey stood up, and Mr. Speedo's cock popped out of his butt. Quentin pulled the model back as Casey got down onto his hands and knees on the floor.

Casey spread his legs apart as Quentin moved Mr. Speedo between his cheeks and slid the giant cock in. Casey was relaxed and lubed, so it entered easily.

Quentin jumped behind the mannequin and pressed his erection into the groove. He entered with one swift movement. His hands clasped the model's hips and pulled him onto his dick. He pushed it away and drove it farther into Casey's ass.

Casey moaned as he backed up onto it. His butt pushed Mr. Speedo onto Quentin's cock.

Quentin guided him off his dick, and Mr. Speedo entered Casey to the hilt. Its balls swung freely between its legs.

"Faster, harder," Casey urged.

Sandwiched between the two men, the mannequin bounced back and forth, gaining speed and depth.

"I'm getting close," Casey warned.

That was all the encouragement Quentin needed. He plowed

into Mr. Speedo and doubled his speed. "Me too."

Casey jacked his cock faster. His balls rose and shot another huge load.

Mr. Speedo continued to hump his butt and forced wave after wave of cum out and onto the floor.

Hearing the wet splat, Quentin's cock released and filled the mannequin's tunnel.

Casey's legs gave out and he landed in his pool of spunk.

Mr. Speedo toppled and landed on top of him, followed by Quentin, cock buried to its root.

They lay in a pile for several minutes, unable to move.

Quentin pushed up and pulled out. He lifted Mr. Speedo off and set him down. He savored the view of his partner's ass. As he bent over to caress it, Quentin's cell phone rang. He looked around and saw it on the floor. It rang again. Dripping from his cock and balls, he walked over to it, picked it up and said, "Hello."

"Did Mr. Rothenberg find you?" Roberta's breathless voice asked.

"He wasn't coming until tomorrow."

"He's early. He came in today. He likes to make surprise visits before he writes a check."

"Where is he?"

"We sent him down to you a half hour ago. He said he'd find you in the new display."

"Shit," Quentin uttered, and scrambled to pick up his clothing. "Get dressed now," he ordered Casey, then spoke again to Roberta. "He's not here, are you sure you sent him to the right display?"

"He hasn't found you yet? He left here about thirty minutes ago. I called to warn you, but you didn't pick up."

"Oh, fuck." Quentin looked down the hallway. He flipped

his phone shut and slowly started to walk out of the locker room. "Mr. Rothenberg? Are you there?"

Casey gasped as he pulled his briefs over his ass.

The mannequin lay on its side. Cum seeped out of its mouth and its bubble butt. Small pools covered the tiled floor.

Mr. Rothenberg stepped out from around the corner. He struggled to zip up his fly.

Quentin relaxed as he spotted a creamy white spot on the floor behind him. "Did you enjoy your sneak attack?"

Mr. Rothenberg's face flushed and he said, "So is this the display that you're planning on installing?"

Quentin froze. Maybe he had misread Mr. Rothenberg. "I... we got carried away for the moment. It won't happen again."

"So, your performance won't be repeated?"

At home, hell yeah, but at work... Quentin thought. "I'm sorry," was all he said.

"Don't be. Do you know how many boring displays I've seen? Do you know how many I've even paid for? I want this one to be hot, controversial, banned from children."

"But sir, this is a public building."

"I don't care. I'm paying for this display, and I want it NC-17."

Casey adjusted his clothing and joined them. He handed Quentin his shirt and pants. He stepped in front of his partner and asked, "How would you like to see this display?"

Mr. Rothenberg walked into the shower room and untied the football player's laces on his pants. He reached into the jock and pulled it down, freeing the mannequin's cock. He pulled it out and let it dangle. He positioned the arm as if he was jacking off.

"I see what you're going for, and I know I can do that." Casey smiled.

Quentin finished dressing behind him and stepped forward. "We can do that." His face still flushed red.

Mr. Rothenberg stepped over to the naked mannequin standing in the corner. "What will he be wearing?"

Casey shrugged his shoulders. "We ran out of uniforms."

"Maybe he can be naked in the shower?"

"Great idea," Casey said.

"But before you do that..." His voice trailed off.

"Yes?" Quentin asked.

"I would like to borrow him for the night."

"Borrow? Oh, yeah, sure. Why don't we bring him to your car through the delivery door?

"Perfect. I'll send my driver around in ten minutes." He extended his hand to Casey. "Thank you." He turned to Quentin and shook his also. "I'll be in tomorrow at one, and the check and new contract will be signed." Mr. Rothenberg turned, adjusted his fly one more time and pointed to the floor. "You may want to clean that up." And he walked away.

Quentin walked over to the naked mannequin and picked him out. Casey grabbed the towel and wrapped it around his waist. "Makes it more fun to unwrap him." Casey smiled as he helped Quentin carry the model down the hallway. "I have one question for you."

Quentin switched his hand position and asked, "What?"

"Why did you give him this one to take to his hotel?"

"He wasn't being used in the display."

"I know, but maybe we could've taken him home with us...."

Quentin stopped and set the model down. He waved his hand back at the display. "We have all of these to pick from, who needs this one tonight?"

Casey kissed him. "I love the way you think, and I hope this display is here for a very long time."

"Maybe we'll have to make this a permanent display."

"Maybe."

QUEEN
INTRIGUE

D. Fostalove

I stepped into the smoothie shop on Peachtree across from Woodruff Park. Scanning the crowd of GSU students and business professionals milling about, I closed my umbrella and strode forward in a pair of black, midcalf, heeled boots and stopped behind a balding man waiting to be served. I bopped to the music flowing through my headphones and gazed at the menu.

As I waited, I felt something brush against my forearm. I glanced back to see a man several inches taller than me with shoulder-length locks pulled back. Solidly built, with a friendly smile, he was the color of a Sacagawea dollar. He had large, brown eyes and was dressed in stonewashed jeans, a black button-down shirt and Timberland boots.

"Excuse me." His eyes scanned my face and lingered on my lips.

"No problem." I stepped forward in line.

When I reached the counter, the barista gave her customary greeting and asked for my order. "I'll have a pomegranate-blueberry smoothie."

The barista set my drink down moments later and rang up my purchase. As I pulled out my wallet, the man standing behind me reached around and slapped a ten dollar bill onto the counter. I looked over my shoulder and removed one of my ear buds. "Uh, what are you doing?"

"Paying for our drinks."

"I can pay for my own, thanks." I pulled a five from my wallet. He grabbed my hand, preventing me from passing the bill to the cashier.

"I want what he has," he said, before looking at me. "For real, I got it."

When he released my hand, I stuffed the bill and wallet into my pocket and placed my headphones back on. Grabbing my drink, I looked at the man and caught him nodding his approval while he gave me the onceover. I took a sip of the smoothie as he reached around me to retrieve his drink.

"I like," he mouthed, referring to the dark green jumpsuit I had on that buttoned down the front. It was similar to the coveralls mechanics and firemen wore.

Pressed for time, I looked around him, hoping he'd get the hint and step aside. Instead he stood planted in the middle of the floor eyeing me while sucking his blended drink through a red straw.

I read his lips as they moved. "What's your name?"

"Seneca."

I removed one bud to hear him repeat my name. On his lips, it sounded like honey drizzled over a biscuit fresh from the oven: smooth, sweet and sapid. I contained the urge to smile, simply nodding, as I waited for him to say something else or move so I could head back to work. Instead he reached for my sunglasses and removed them.

I switched the music off.

"I can't see your eyes," he explained.

"You could've asked me to take them off."

"Oh, my god, that's…" someone in the crowd announced.

He waved at the woman and turned back to me.

"What?" I watched him exploring my body with an acute fascination.

"You're dressed femme but when you open your mouth…"

"I'm all man." I finished his sentence.

"Yes."

I started to tell him I wasn't the stereotypical loud, finger-snapping queen but smiled instead and said, "If you really got to know me, you'd realize I'm the *perfect* mix of feminine and masculine.…"

"How can I get to know you?"

"You can't." I grabbed my glasses and sidestepped him to exit. Opening my umbrella, I strolled outside into the pouring rain with him following.

"Do you know who I am?"

"You *used* to be the chief meteorologist for WFOS News." I looked past him to a group of students standing under an awning pointing in our direction. "That doesn't change anything though. I'm still not interested."

"That's cold," he said, and paused before asking me if I was jaded.

"No, I'm not bitter." I leaned forward and whispered. "I just don't have time for men who are obviously on the prowl for a fast, mindless fuck."

"What makes you think I'm looking to sex you?" He rubbed his hairless chin.

"It's in your eyes."

His gaze moved from the area of my chest exposed by an undone top button to meet my eyes. "I'd like to know more about you than what's hiding beneath those coveralls."

"I know how you high-profile men operate. You like to pick queens up late nights, take them to dirty hotels, run through them like sluts and toss them on the curb wherever you found them." I watched the pelting rain soak him as he stood just outside the span of my umbrella. "I'll pass."

He reached into his back pocket, pulled out a business card and held it up. "Let me show you I'm different than the rest."

"Really, I'm flattered," I said, letting the card dangle in his outstretched hand. "But men are no longer a pastime of mine."

My cell phone rang. I pulled it out and brought it to my ear. "Veronica, I'm headed back now. I'll grab the proposals off my desk when I return and meet you in the conference room. Okay?"

"I see you're in a rush," he said, shoving the card into his pocket. "I'll let you go."

"Thanks again for the smoothie." I took another sip.

Just then he snatched the phone from my hand and proceeded to type his number into it. I waited. He dropped the phone into my open palm after saving his info. "Don't make me wait too long."

"Bye, Byron." I darted across the street before the stoplight turned green.

The fill-in receptionist giggled and waved me over as I entered the university's Department of Risk Management. Strolling to her desk, I leaned in and asked, "Why are you grinning like that? Something going on that I haven't heard about yet?"

"Seneca, you didn't tell me you were dating again."

I set my bag on her desk with a raised eyebrow. "I'm not. Why would you think I was?"

She pointed in the direction of my office. I gazed down the

hall through the glass door, seeing several large bouquets of yellow and blue flowers on my desk. I shrugged and walked toward the office, curious to see who had sent them.

Entering the space, I beamed at the three clear vases full of yellow Asiatic lilies and blue irises. Dropping my designer bag, I searched through the bouquets looking for a card and when I found it, I snatched it from its holder and tore it open. Reading the enclosed message, I smiled faintly.

"Who's it from?" the receptionist asked with a clipboard pressed to her chest. I jumped, not realizing she'd been standing in the doorway.

"A secret admirer." I moved my bag and sat.

"It's not Warren apologizing, is it?" Her smile faded and so did mine.

"Has hell frozen over?" I stared again at the printed message. "I need to make a personal call."

As I watched the temp shuffling to the front, I picked up the office phone and dialed the number inside the card. After several rings, Byron answered.

"Do you like the flowers?" he asked without a greeting.

Smiling but not letting him know I was by my tone of voice, I asked flatly, "How did you find out where I worked? Did you follow me the other day?"

He laughed, genuinely amused. "I bet you'd like that, wouldn't you?"

"I've been stalked before. It's not anything I'd like to go through again." I randomly played with the petals of a flower, trying to remember the last time a man had brought me any sentimental gift.

"Tell me you like them."

"I do," I said, thinking he'd never know how much they really meant. "Why are you doing this?"

"I thought they would brighten your day."

I imagined him sitting behind a large desk in an expansive office in the GEMA headquarters building where he currently worked after leaving WFOS, much to the chagrin of viewers. I could see him licking his lips, enjoying the fact I'd admitted to liking the flowers.

"Byron, I have tons of work to do," I said. "I'll have to talk to you later."

"Promise?"

"What?" I moved one of the vases from my immediate work-space.

"Promise me you'll call later."

I stared through the glass door at the receptionist peeking over her desk to see if I was still preoccupied with my conversation. "Why are you pursuing me like this when we both know you could have any man or woman you wanted?"

"Seneca…" I loved hearing him call my name.

"Yes?"

"I'm not interested in just anyone. I'm interested in you."

Blushing, I dismissed the idea that someone as attractive, successful or popular could want something more than sex from a cute, educated queen with expensive tastes who'd sworn off men after a near-fatal six-year relationship. I wanted to tell him I preferred my career over another's affections because I was damaged, like a pair of scuffed Prada pumps, and scared of being abused again. I stopped short, knowing he would hear none of it.

"Are you still there?"

"Yes, I'm here." I shook at visions of Warren choking me to near unconsciousness while brandishing a knife inches from my face as he screamed frantically that he would kill us both before he let me leave him.

"What do I have to do to see you again?" Byron asked. "Hand deliver the flowers next time?"

The idea of him coming to the job frightened and excited me at the same time. "Please don't do that. It would cause a big scene."

"Then go out with me and save us both the spectacle."

I turned the laptop on and searched my bag for the CD I'd saved several reports on. "Byron..."

"Step out with me," he said. "We'll do whatever you like."

Knowing he would keep badgering me until I submitted, I quickly muttered, "I'll think about it and call you later," before insisting I had to get off the phone to start on the day's business.

While I was typing feverishly, the office phone rang. I glanced over and saw the receptionist's name flash across the screen. I ignored it and continued typing, trying to finish a document for the dean before three o'clock. As I proofread the paragraphs, the receptionist rang again.

Snatching up the handset, I said, "Tessa, this better be important."

She was panting and stammering over her words. "You need to come out here. Now."

"Why?" I was glad she'd returned from maternity leave but not in the mood for office gossip.

"Come...out...here." She sounded like she was hyperventilating.

I set the phone down and stepped around my desk, pulling the office door aside. Byron stood at the other end of the hall just beyond the receptionist's desk, sporting a cranberry sweater and black slacks. He held a large bag at his side and smiled down at Tessa who fanned herself with a takeout menu. She kept saying she couldn't believe it was him and how she only watched the news for his weather report.

Shocked, I said, "I thought I asked you not to come here."

He turned at the sound of my voice. "You look nice today. How are you feeling?"

I waved him over, seeing several women gathered behind Tessa's desk as I approached. Holding a hand to my forehead, I said to myself, "Lord, I can't believe this is happening."

"He's even more gorgeous in person," one of the women said. "Can I take a picture with you?"

"No pictures." I reached under Byron's arm and yanked him forward with as much strength as I could muster. He laughed at my effort to usher him along. Once inside my office, I slammed the door and stared at him angrily, yelling, "I can't believe you're doing this. Are you freaking serious?"

"Calm down," Byron said, attempting to pat my shoulder. "I'm not trying to cause any trouble."

"Then what do you call what you're doing right now? You have everyone in my office going gaga over you. I don't have time for this hoopla." I could see his pectoral muscles flexing underneath his sweater. Trying not to get distracted by them, I moved my gaze upward to his face with its wide smile plastered across it. It was infectious. I wanted to smile along with him but refused, knowing word had spread throughout the office like legs at a DL sex party; not just any man, but this man had strolled in leisurely and was now behind closed doors with me.

He laughed, running a hand through his locks. "I'm sorry."

I frowned. "I'm not amused by this, so stop laughing."

He held up the bag. "Hopefully this will make you feel better."

I reluctantly reached for the bag while glaring at him, completely frustrated. Dumping the box inside onto my desk,

I pulled the lid off and immediately gasped. Inside was a pair of bronze Giuseppe boots with all-over strap detailing. I knew immediately he'd spent at least a thousand for them.

"I figured you were about a size nine in women's," he said, smiling. "Try them on and let's see."

I pulled off one of my stiletto boots and slid into the shoe. It fit perfectly. "I love them."

"It's my pleasure." He took a seat behind my desk and spun around in the chair. "So..."

"What?" I couldn't take my eyes off the shoe as I strutted around the office.

Byron remained silent as he watched me pace the room.

"Seneca, I find you very intriguing."

I stopped sauntering and stared at him. "You're intrigued by the queen, huh?"

"Yeah." He eyed me intently.

I broke his gaze and stared down at the shoe.

"Didn't I tell you I'd come to your job if you didn't call me back?" He leaned forward in the chair and placed both elbows on my desk. "I wasn't playing."

I heard giggles outside the door. I moved toward it and swung the door open. Tessa and three female coworkers stood on the other side, cupping hands over their mouths at being caught. "Move from around my door with that snickering. There's nothing funny going on in here."

The women scattered like thieves hearing police sirens. I closed the door and turned to see Byron had moved from the chair and now stood in front of me. I stepped backward, bumping into the door, rattling the closed blinds. Being inches from him made me suddenly realize this was the first time since Warren that I'd been alone with a man. The thought unnerved me.

"How much longer do I have to pursue you before you give in?" Byron asked.

"You're just not going to take no for an answer, are you?"

He shook his head and reached to touch my shaved face. "I'm used to getting what I want and now that I can't, I want it even more."

"Good." I stepped around him and grabbed the door handle, pulling the door open. "Now you must go. There are several things that require my immediate attention."

"Things more important than me?"

"Yes, things more important than you."

Byron poked his bottom lip out. "You're kicking me out just like that after I came all the way from Douglasville with gifts? Can I at least get a thank-you kiss to hold me over until I see you again?"

Unable to contain my smile, I asked, "Are you serious?"

He placed his hand over mine and gently closed the door. Leaning down, he pecked my lips with his soft pink lips. I wanted to press REWIND and have him kiss me like that over and over again. "I'm glad you like the shoes."

"Byron?" I said as he pulled the door open, his hand still over mine. "I'll call you...soon."

Mouthing, "I'll be waiting," he stepped into the hallway and disappeared around the corner that led out of the office. Standing in the doorway long after he'd gone, in mismatched shoes, I relived the gentle peck, loving how he kissed me good-bye.

Lifting my head from the desk, I glared at the phone with its annoying ring and snatched it up. "Risk Management, Seneca speaking."

Byron's voice invaded my ear. "I figured you'd still be at work."

"What time is it?" I rubbed my eyes, realizing night had fallen and the office was dark but for the glow from the computer screen. "I'm late, aren't I?"

"It's almost seven but that's all right."

I pressed the speakerphone button, grabbed my bag and saved several open documents on the computer before shutting it down. "I'm headed out now. Give me thirty minutes to run home and freshen up. Then I'll meet you at the restaurant."

I climbed off the elevator in the parking deck and readjusted both my handbag and laptop case. Strutting down the aisle searching the sparse lot for my car, I noticed a man leaned on the hood of a blue sports car toward the back. I eyed him suspiciously and clutched my bags. He wore a plaid gold and brown button-down shirt, khakis and tan loafers.

"So you're going to act like you don't see me?" The man's voice echoed throughout the deck.

"Byron?" I squinted to see him. "What are you doing here?"

"I was banking on you being late or canceling." He leaned into the blue Porsche two-door coupe and pulled out a plastic bag. I could smell his cologne as he breezed by. It was strong, fresh but not overpowering. "So I brought dinner to you. I hope you like Chu Chu's Chinese takeout."

I eyeballed him, wondering if he'd called the office to ask Tessa where I liked to eat. Chu Chu's was my ultimate favorite Chinese spot. I nodded my approval as Byron reached for my bags with his free hand and tossed them into the compact trunk. Slamming it shut, he grabbed my hand and led me to the passenger side, where he opened the door and allowed me to climb inside. "Where are we headed?"

Jumping into the driver's side, he started the car and put it into reverse without a word. As we wound round and round the deck toward the top, I glanced at his locks braided in a cornrow style. Reaching the top deck, Byron stopped, placed the car in park and climbed out. I hopped out and met him where he stood at the hood. He dug into the food bag and pulled out a carton, handing it over. He then pulled another for himself before passing me a plastic-wrapped fork, knife and napkin set.

"Beef and broccoli for you and Hunan shrimp for me."

Byron ripped his fork from its wrapper and dug into his carton of food. I followed, sitting on the hood next to him as I stared randomly at the skyscrapers surrounding us. The cool fall breeze calmed my nerves as I hungrily consumed the only meal I'd had for the day.

As we ate, Byron said randomly, "I know you're wondering how someone like me could be interested in someone like you...."

"I've thought about it before." I looked into the cloudless sky.

"You can walk around town in a pair of stilettos with your head held high, and not think twice about it. I admire that about you." He reached over and with a finger under my chin, turned me to face him. "I haven't come across anyone, male or female, more attractive than you. From your eyes to your lips to your smooth skin, you're on point in every way. I love that cute little walk you have and the way you talk, even when you're getting feisty with me."

No man had ever admitted to being impressed with my courage to leave home dressed as I did. I chewed the food still in my mouth and stared at the building across from us with several floors still fully lit, wondering if Byron was attempting to use flattery as a way to slide between my thighs.

He reached over and pulled the fork and carton of half-eaten food from my grasp. "Seneca, what's wrong? Did I say something you didn't like?"

"No," I muttered.

"I'm not going to hurt you."

I knew he wasn't going to, but I still felt uneasy. I stood. He followed, moving in front of me. Unexpectedly he threw his large arms around me, pulling me in. The sudden embrace startled me and simultaneously comforted me. Something about him made me feel secure, wanted, needed, desired.

Byron whispered again into my ear, "I won't hurt you. I promise."

When I felt his hand running along my lower back, I flinched. "I like you, Byron, but…"

He silenced me with a kiss so simple and sweet it dissolved all doubt about him. Standing on tiptoes, I kissed him back. I wrapped both arms around his neck as he held me around my waist, our kisses transforming into something more passionate and prolonged. I felt his tongue slide into my mouth as I closed my eyes.

As we kissed, Byron's hands found their way under both my teal oxford shirt and T-shirt. Warm and soft, his hands traced from my ribs to my hips and back up again, eventually grazing my chest and erect nipples. I flinched as he ran circles around them with his thumbs. While he slowly caressed my body, I unbuttoned his shirt. He removed his hands momentarily, allowing the fabric to fall off his shoulders onto the ground.

Staring at his toned, hairless chest with its perky brown nipples, I instinctively leaned forward with open mouth and wrapped my lips around one while clenching his other meaty pectoral muscle with my hand. He moaned, his hands fumbling under my shirt again. As I alternated between sucking his nipples, my idle hands undid his belt and unzipped his khakis, the fabric sliding down his thick golden thighs into a heap atop his loafers.

Looking up at Byron as I kissed my way down his chest and stomach to the trail of hair that led from his belly button to the cotton band of his underwear, I realized he was staring toward the large windows around us. I knew he was thinking people in the high-rises would see every moment of our intimate encounter.

"Let them watch." I shifted his face away from the windows and back to me. Between us, I could see his dick expanding in his boxer-briefs, snaking seductively up and around his thigh.

Smiling, he leaned down to where I sat on the hood and kissed me. I reached down and slid my hand into his briefs, my fingers traveling through his soft, curly pubic hair. Finding his flashlight-thick dick throbbing in the underbrush anxiously awaiting my touch, I gripped it and flipped it out. I stroked it gently as we kissed and ran my thumb over the head that was wet with excitement. Easing away from Byron's intense kisses, I eyed his member as I trailed the pulsating vein that zigzagged along the top.

I attempted to nudge him away so I could lower myself but Byron didn't budge. Still slowly stroking him, I looked up. "You don't want me to...?"

"It's all about pleasing you tonight," he said calmly, removing my hand from his erect dick. I wanted to run my tongue up and down it like it was the sweetest thing I'd ever tasted while I played with his large muscadine-shaped balls but he gently removed my hand the second time I grabbed for it.

Wedged between his throbbing dick and the car hood, I realized I'd long forgotten the concept of pleasure. All my encounters with Warren had been reduced to him pounding me from behind with rabid hostility. I wanted to tell Byron he could do anything he liked as long as it didn't include violence or him calling me a bitch, whore, or faggot but decided against it and suggested we do whatever came natural.

Nodding, Byron brought me to my feet and slowly removed

both my shirts, tossing them on the hood. "Take off your pants but leave on the boots."

I pulled my belt off and removed my slacks, standing naked before him in snakeskin boots. He surveyed me with great enthusiasm, licking his lips and stroking himself.

"Turn around. Place your hands on the hood."

I spun around while Byron lowered himself behind me. I could feel his breath on the backs of my thighs before I felt his tongue lapping them like a kitten to a bowl of milk. Inching closer to my ass, he bit one of my cheeks.

"If you stick your tongue out, I'll let you taste it."

He opened his mouth and flicked his tongue out in anticipation as I crept backward into the salivating protrusion. Parting my cheeks with both hands, Byron fervently circled my anus before prodding it with his tongue. Throwing my head back toward the sky, I moaned loudly as he increased his tongue's movements. Without me noticing, he replaced his tongue with a single pudgy digit as he inserted it slowly at first and then entered and exited me with a pace that made me shudder.

"Enough," I cried, sucking my middle finger, my knees weak. "I want to feel *it*."

Byron searched his pants pockets frantically for a condom and when he found one, he soaked my backside with his saliva before rolling it on. "Ready?"

I nodded and placed both palms on the hood, bracing myself. Feeling his hot muscle poking between my cheeks searching for the entrance, I exhaled deeply awaiting it. Finding the spot, he deliberately pressed onward with caution, knowing his ten, thick inches weren't a small feat to take. As he slowly pulled out that first time, my tightness gripped him like a Chinese finger trap. I wanted to feel him in the worst way but the pain sent jolts through my body.

As I controlled my breathing and focused on anything other than him stuffing his oversized brick of a dick inside me, Byron rubbed my back and assured me he'd be gentle. My ass tightened from the sheer shock of it all when he slid back into me and out again. After a few, slow steady strokes, I forced him to stop. I pointed to the hood and told him to lie down. Hopefully, a change in position would help.

Climbing atop him, I held the massive piece of flesh in my hand while I lowered myself onto it. We stared at each other the entire time, him biting his lip, me holding his muscular shoulders as I relaxed and began to bounce up and down on him after I'd gotten used to being penetrated again.

As the thrusts of Byron's hips quickened, I lay down on his sweaty chest and kissed his neck. He wrapped one arm around my back and gripped my ass with the other as he slammed it back onto his dick with each stroke. Moaning into his ear, I bit his earlobe and clawed at the windshield in a futile attempt to pry myself away from his endless inches hitting spots deep inside.

With every bit of strength I could summon, I broke free from Byron's strong arm around my back and placed a hand on his chest, signaling I wanted to take over. He stopped and rubbed the sweat from my chest, licking it from his fingers. I sat straight up, closed my eyes and gyrated to my own rhythm, a series of figure eights and zeros in no particular order. Whatever felt good, whatever generated more prolonged groans from him.

I felt him flexing, his long dick stretching my insides. I knew he was ready to explode by the way his eyes rolled back and how he kept whispering my name. I quickened my movements and leaned forward, kissing him passionately. He gripped my ass with both hands as I wiggled on him.

He mumbled inaudibly while thrusting himself into me.

Feeling close to coming, I started stroking myself. Byron knocked my hand away and with the sweat from our bodies, jerked me while I twisted atop him, my face contorted in pleasure.

Byron stammered as he moaned my name. I kept riding him relentlessly, feeling the buildup in my sac. He kept jerking me quicker until white globs exploded onto his stomach and chest. I could feel him throbbing inside and knew he was coming too.

Aching and drained, I fell onto him and wheezed. Lazily, Byron threw both arms around my back and held me. We lay there in the sticky mess I'd made, our hearts pounding next to each other, our ragged breaths eventually quieting.

"Will I see you again?" I whispered. "I mean after tonight."

As I lay in his arms, the warmth of his body nullifying the cool breeze on my back, I wondered if all the queens who bedded these types of men asked the same silly question afterward.

"I should be asking you that."

Calmed by his words, I snuggled up in his arms with a slight smile and closed my eyes.

BRAND-NEW DANCE

Stephen Osborne

"We're in a rut."

Reluctantly, Marty lowered the entertainment section of the *Indianapolis News* and cast a baleful look at his partner. Barely missing a beat, he replied, "We're not in a rut." Marty adjusted the newspaper, sipped his coffee and returned to his reading.

Dan reached across the table and snapped the paper out of Marty's hands, ignoring the snort of protest his boyfriend emitted. "I say we're in a rut, and goddamn it, that means we're in a rut."

Marty's smile held a hint of indulgence. After ten years of cohabiting with Daniel, he was used to such outbursts. "Okay, we're in a rut. Ruts happen. You live with anyone as long we we've lived together and you hit ruts every now and then. Big deal."

Dan's shoulders slumped and he pouted, another typical Dan mannerism. "This is a rut years in the making. We're getting too used to each other. We've become mired in routine."

Trying not to roll his eyes, Marty took a long sip of coffee before replying, making sure he gave himself time so that he could at least sound concerned over Dan's latest bit of drama. "You know I love you. I may not say it enough, but..."

"I'm not fishing for an I Love You," Dan said.

"What, then?"

Dan sighed as he pushed away his breakfast plate, his eggs and bacon hardly touched. "Every day is the same. We sit here at the kitchen table for breakfast every morning. You have coffee. I have tea. We both have bacon and eggs. You read the entertainment section of the paper first, then the front page. I just read the comics and watch 'The View.'"

"Okay," Marty said with a shrug, "tomorrow I'll have tea instead."

Dan flashed his lover a twisted grin. "Funny. Our sex life is the same as well. You turn out the lights, fumble around on the nightstand for condoms and lube, and then you jump on top of me and screw my ass..."

"It's a really nice ass," Marty remarked, hoping to placate Dan.

"...and ten minutes later we're done. You roll over and I turn on my book light to read a chapter of Nora Roberts."

Marty sighed. He started to pick up his coffee mug but realized it was now empty, which prompted another sigh. He really didn't want to continue the conversation but could see no easy way out of it. He contemplated picking the newspaper back up, but he knew that would only fuel Dan's mood further. The truth was that, while he could concede that they had maybe fallen into a routine (not a rut, which had negative connotations), he liked the way their days had become a pattern. He liked seeing Dan's rumpled blond hair over the top of his newspaper in the morning. If he read something unpleasant, all he had to do was glance over and see his boyfriend's somewhat chubby face and he felt better. And, damn it, he *liked* fucking Dan's tight ass. What was wrong with that? A thought suddenly hit Marty and he reached across the table and took Dan's hand in his.

"I know what this is about," he said.

"Oh, really?"

Marty nodded. "You want more foreplay. Tonight I'll give you a nice, sexy massage when we get into bed."

Dan snatched his hand away and folded his arms across his chest. "You haven't been listening to a word I've said. We need a major shake-up to rekindle our relationship."

Throwing his hands up to signal submission, Marty chuckled uneasily. "Fine. I'm sure you're right. I just don't know what we can do about it. It's just something we'll snap out of. We always do."

Dan's face softened a little as some of the fire went out of him, now that Marty had given in. "Do you trust me?" he asked.

"You know I do. Always have."

With a slight and somewhat mischievous smile, Dan said, "Then come home for lunch. Let them know you might be late coming back, if you make it back at all this afternoon."

Marty raised an eyebrow. "What do you have in mind?"

"That would spoil the surprise, now, wouldn't it?

"Okay." Marty shrugged. "We're going through a slack time at the office right now anyway. Taking the afternoon off won't be a big deal at all." He fingered the newspaper tentatively. "Can I get back to my reading now?"

Beaming with satisfaction, Dan replied, "By all means. I have to start making my plans anyway. Just don't forget. Home for lunch."

"I won't forget," Marty muttered. The newspaper was already raised. He grunted his thanks as Dan poured him a second cup of coffee.

* * *

As he pulled into a parking spot in front of their apartment building, Marty found himself smiling. While he thought Dan was being his typical drama-queen self, there was no denying that their sex life could use some sprucing up. Any couple that had been together as long as he and Dan had was bound to have a few low spots.

Marty knew exactly what Dan's solution was going to be. Marty would be met at the door by a cherub-faced Dan wearing nothing but a skimpy little Speedo. And that was cool. The sight of Dan in a Speedo was sure to get an arousal out of Marty. They'd have some hot, heavy sex right there in the living room before moving into the bedroom for a more tender and loving second round. And things would be back on track.

The thought of Dan in his Speedo made Marty hurry out of his car. At their door he fumbled with his keys before finally getting it open. He frowned slightly when there was no Dan or a Speedo waiting for him. The apartment was dark. Dan had closed all the curtains, which Marty had expected. After all, they didn't really need any neighbors going by catching sight of Dan bent over the couch as Marty humped his tight little ass. But where was Dan? Marty listened, puzzled. He'd been so sure of his Speedo scenario that he was somewhat caught off guard. What was Dan up to? He called out his lover's name. Marty's voice sounded too loud in the quiet apartment.

Had Dan, who had been so worked up about the whole "rut" thing only hours earlier, forgotten? Was he having one of his Blond Days, where he forgot everything in his spacey but utterly adorable way? Marty grinned to himself. He'd really have to give Dan hell over this.

He almost turned to leave when a sound from the bedroom door made him pause. "Dan?" he called out as he craned his neck to get a good look down the hallway.

The bedroom door opened slowly. Just as slowly Dan emerged and the sight made Marty's jaw drop. Dan was dressed in leather: Leather straps crossing his chest. Black leather shorts adorned with studs at the waistline. White socks that barely showed over the top of gleaming leather boots. And in Dan's right hand was a short whip, which he cracked menacingly in the air.

"Holy shit," Marty murmured.

Dan was attempting to look stern, but he couldn't keep the hint of a smile from crossing his face. "You like what you see, boy?" He spoke in a lower register than normal, the words coming out as a sexy growl.

"Like?" Marty shook his head. "I'm still in shock. Where the hell did you get all this stuff?"

"Went shopping," was the terse reply. Again the whip cracked. "Now I suggest you close the door unless you want Old Lady Anderson across the hall to have a heart attack when she takes her poodle out for his afternoon walk."

Marty closed the door.

Dan strode down the hall, his boots sounding incredibly loud on their tile floor. He came right up to Marty, not stopping until their chests were pressed together. Dan, several inches shorter, had to look up into his boyfriend's eyes. "You didn't answer my question. You like?"

Running a finger along one of the straps that crisscrossed Dan's chest, Marty replied, "Yeah. I like a lot."

"Wait until you see the rest."

Marty's eyebrows shot up. "There's more?"

"Oh, yeah." Dan grabbed Marty by the lapels and began to haul him down the hall toward the bedroom. Marty, giggling like a little kid, went willingly, wondering what more surprises awaited him.

With the blinds down there wasn't a lot of light in the hall, and it took a moment for Marty's eyes to adjust when Dan opened the bedroom door. Even then he wasn't sure he was seeing right. Surely this couldn't be something Dan set up. Not the Dan who, during the first few months they dated, couldn't make love with the lights on and still to this day refused to watch gay porn because "it was dirty."

Suspended from the ceiling by some heavy-duty bolts was a leather sling.

Marty couldn't help but gape like an idiot at the sight. "Holy mother of pearl, where the hell did you get that?"

Dan couldn't keep the grin off his face. "There's this little sex shop down on Massachusetts Avenue. Who knew? Anyway, it came in red or black leather. I thought black looked more butch and dangerous, though. What do you think?"

"I think I need to find out what you've done with the real Dan. I think I've come home to a science fiction version of my life," Marty said, giving the sling a tentative swing. It seemed sturdy enough. "Well, I guess if we want to shake up our sex life, we might as well go all out. So you get in this and…"

"Oh, no." Dan cracked the whip again, coming dangerously close to Marty's behind. "The sling is for you, buddy-boy."

Surprise and a hint of panic showed in Marty's eyes. When they had first become a couple, the two had tried every sexual position and combination they could think of, but after a while they had settled into a comfortable pattern with Marty being the top and Dan the bottom. Marty couldn't remember when he'd last taken it up the ass, and the thought worried him a little. He looked at Dan. "You're kidding, right?"

"Nope."

The whip cracked again, this time actually making contact with Marty's posterior. Marty yelped and did an impromptu dance, cupping his stinging buttocks in his hands. "Ouch, you bitch. That hurt!" It actually did hurt, but just the fact that the injury was inflicted by sweet, calm little Dan made Marty laugh even as he rubbed the wound.

The color drained from Dan's cheeks. "Oh, I'm so sorry, baby." He pulled Marty close, hugging him tight.

That did it. Marty nearly fell on the floor laughing. The sight of Dan in full leather regalia, standing next to a leather sling, whip in hand, apologizing for causing the minor sting was too much for Marty. Dan's high-pitched giggle soon mingled with Marty's hearty guffaws and it was several moments before either could speak. When words could actually be formed, Marty said, "I think it ruins the illusion if you apologize when you whip me."

With a twinkle in his eye, Dan snapped the whip. "Then you'd better get your clothes off real fast and get in that sling before you get another."

Marty complied.

Soon not only was he naked in the sling, but his wrists and ankles were bound in restraints as well. If he had been in that position with anyone other than Dan he'd have been worried, but he trusted his lover to the end of the universe. Marty hadn't noticed that the leather shorts Dan was wearing had snaps, but as he watched, Dan opened a flap to reveal his hard cock. As Dan lubed up, he said, "I thought about getting you a gag, but I know you've got a bad gag reflex and I didn't want to go too far. Plus I'd already spent a ton on the rest of this stuff."

"I'd have drawn the line there anyway. I can't even go to the dentist without having a major panic attack."

Dan positioned himself between Marty's spread legs and pressed the head of his cock against Marty's hole. Marty took a deep breath, fearing the jolt of pain he thought was surely coming. There was some discomfort, but the thunder strike of agony he was expecting never came. *Maybe laughing ourselves silly relaxed me enough,* Marty thought. Whatever the reason, Dan's hard prick was entering his ass with relative ease.

When it was all in, Marty let out the breath he hadn't realized he'd been holding. "Oh," he whispered, "that feels so good."

Dan suddenly smacked Marty's ass hard with the flat of his hand. Impulsively Marty jerked, but he could barely wiggle in the restraints. The impact made his ass tighten around Dan's cock. Marty, to his surprise, found that he was more than a little titillated by this new, bold Dan.

"Yeah, you like me fucking you, don't you?" Dan growled as he began pumping his dick into Marty's ass.

Marty was kept from answering by another smack on his ass. Dan knew him well and was obviously reading his body language and knew how much Marty was getting turned on by the new, rough Dan. Of course, Marty's untouched yet near-to-bursting cock was a sure sign of Marty's enjoyment.

More pumping. More slaps on the ass. Helpless in the sling, Marty could only moan with pleasure, and if Mrs. Anderson really was out in the hall preparing to take Mr. Snuffles out for his afternoon stroll she probably could hear him. Not that he cared.

Dan began to sweat as he pounded his lover's butt. "I'm gonna shoot," he muttered.

"Give it to me, baby," Marty replied.

Just in time Dan pulled his dick out of Marty and sent a long stream of cum across Marty's abdomen. After several body-shaking spurts, Dan grasped Marty's aching cock and began to stroke the swollen monster. It didn't take much. Marty let out a howl and suddenly his semen was mixing with Dan's in sticky pools all over his stomach.

* * *

After cleanup, Dan broke open a bottle of wine. The two snuggled on the bed, sipping chardonnay and occasionally kissing. Both of them kept looking over at the sling.

"That was fun," Marty said. "Let's leave it up. Later, you can take your turn in the thing."

Dan chuckled and ran his hand through Marty's thick, dark hair. "Sure thing. And aren't Ben and Tommy coming over tonight?"

The implication caught Marty off guard. He stared at Dan but could tell his lover was totally serious. "Wow," he said. "When you make up your mind to shake up a routine, you really shake it up, don't you?"

Dan laughed and the two fell back on the bed, nearly spilling their wine. Marty's bare foot kicked out and clipped the sling slightly, making it sway rhythmically.

LINE OF SIGHT

Nathan Burgoine

Tate's back on Saturday," Johnny said.

I looked up. Johnny was sitting across from me, pouting, arms crossed. We were at the coffee shop where we'd met. He was one of the "beautiful gays," as I liked to think of them. His hair was a frosted blond, his teeth capped, his body designed by hours on a treadmill and his skin tanned in booths.

Had I not saved his life, I doubt he'd have deigned to speak with me.

"Tate is Bill's roommate, right?"

Johnny nodded, and a flash of green covered my vision, with a mild sense of being an outsider. Jealousy. Bill was Johnny's boyfriend. Bill was a soldier—currently stationed at the local base, though I hadn't met him—and he shared a two-bedroom condo with Tate, another soldier. They'd known each other for years. Since they were often shipped elsewhere at different times, the shared condo worked to their financial advantage. When I'd first met Johnny, he had been frustrated by how Bill and Tate were "each other's left testicle" but Tate had deployed a week later. Johnny had dropped the topic after that, except for expressing annoyance when a postcard or letter arrived requesting Bill mail something to Afghanistan.

"I'm sure Bill's happy," I said carefully.

Johnny rolled his eyes. "Over the fucking moon. I swear he likes Tate more than me."

I said nothing. I'd literally bumped into Johnny in line at this coffee shop months ago. I'd had one of my flashes and blurted out: "Don't get in the car. There's going to be an accident."

I'd scared the hell out of him. He'd called me a freak when I'd described the car and a nighttime drive, and he'd stormed out, *sans* coffee, visibly disturbed. He was supposed to have driven to Detroit that evening with a friend. He'd backed out. His friend had scoffed and gone without him. The friend was sideswiped and ended up upside down in a ditch, the passenger side of his car mostly crushed and his right leg broken.

Johnny had camped out at the coffee shop waiting for me to show up again after that.

"You saved my life," he'd said. "The least I can do is get you a decent haircut."

I'd never really had a friend like Johnny before. I'd not had many friends, period—it's hard to maintain a friendship when you randomly know stuff they'd rather you didn't—but I quickly learned that wouldn't be a problem with Johnny. Johnny had one topic of interest: himself. As much as that could grate on my nerves, it was sort of relaxing. And sometimes when I was with him, I got an image of myself, smiling. Somehow, it seemed, Johnny would bring me happiness. He certainly added a social quality I'd never really enjoyed. He had enough energy for two people, enough attitude for four, and it never dawned on him that other people wouldn't find him fascinating, so they did.

"...For his birthday," Johnny was saying.

"Sorry?" I said. Red jerseys flashed behind my eyes.

"Hockey game," Johnny said, with a tone usually reserved for "pedophile." "Bill got tickets for a hockey game for all three of us on Monday night, which is Tate's birthday, aka the second coming of Christ."

I felt my lips quirk. "I like hockey."

"I'm being a bitch," Johnny said. "But you can't blame me. Bill isn't Bill when Tate's around. He's Bill-and-Tate. It's next to impossible to get him alone."

I smiled. "They sound close. I imagine Don't Ask, Don't Tell makes things hard." I didn't have trouble imagining having to hide a part of myself—being psychic often stayed a secret—but at least they knew each other. Having someone who knew was wonderful.

"Yeah," Johnny said. "It sucks. We can't go to clubs, no parades, and no events."

"Ah," I said. Trust Johnny to think I was thinking of how difficult it would be for him, not his boyfriend. "Rough on Bill and Tate, too."

Johnny shrugged and sipped his latte. "Probably. But that doesn't fix the problem. Tate needs a life, and..." His voice trailed off, and he looked at me, eyes filling with calculation.

I leaned back. "What?"

"Saturday night, what are you doing?" Johnny asked me, then shook his head. "Never mind. Saturday night, you're not doing anything. You never are. Come," he said, and rose.

"I'm not done with my coffee," I said, stung. But Johnny was right. I didn't go out—I don't like crowds.

"Too bad. We got a lot of work to do before Saturday."

"We do?" I said, blinking. Pulses of images were flashing behind my eyes, but they were changing too fast to catch.

"You need a new shirt. Something green, that works for you. Some good pants, preferably black. I'm sure I can get Bryan to squeeze you in for a trim... Seriously, when are you going to start caring about your hair?"

"Probably never," I said, rising. "Why the makeover?"

"You're going to meet Tate, and you're going to use that flash of yours to help me figure out who he should be with."

Mentally, I added a definition for images that were too fast to track: a big mistake.

Bill's condo wasn't far from where I lived, but Johnny picked me up anyway. As always, Johnny kept up most of the conversation on the short drive there. I felt strange in the designer shirt—green—and the slick pants—black—and the new shoes—shiny. But I did like what Bryan had done to my hair, which was understated and short. I'd never stand out in a crowd like Johnny did. I had brown hair, hazel eyes (which really did look nice when I wore green), and a strong chin, but mostly I blended. I could have been that guy next door. Oh, I guess I was handsome enough, and I kept fit running. If I wanted to get laid, I managed it. Being psychic helped me figure out who wanted to take me home, though going to the bars was a kind of psychic torture.

"So, do your thing when you shake Tate's hand. Figure out who it is I need to track down to get Tate out of my life. Hallelujah, and praise Jesus!"

"It's not that simple," I said. "It doesn't work on demand. I've told you that."

"You said usually it's the strongest the first time you touch someone," Johnny said.

That was true. "Yeah, but..." I sighed. "I'll try."

Johnny shook my shoulder. "Good boy."

I caught an image of Johnny, naked and sweaty, bent over on a bed with a wide-shouldered blond man fucking him with wild abandon. The man had a tattoo on the back of his left shoulder—I couldn't make it out—and tacky black silk sheets. The big blond said, "Good boy, you like that, boy?"

I coughed, and blinked rapidly. Apparently Johnny was in for a good time with Bill after all.

"So how many people will be there?" I asked.

"Just us and them," Johnny said. "We're having a barbecue." He sighed. "Tate likes steak."

I looked out the window for the rest of the trip, while I heard about the foods Tate liked that Bill had cooked because Tate missed them.

Bill wasn't the big blond guy. When Johnny started to work his key in the lock, a muscular man opened the door. I assumed he was Tate, but Johnny said, "Hey, babe!" and jumped at him. They shared a kiss while Bill grabbed Johnny's ass and gave it a squeeze with both hands, physically lifting him into the doorway and pressing him against the wall.

Blond he wasn't, but he *was* very wide shouldered, and I had an honest moment of confusion, having assumed the man from my brief X-rated vision was going to be Bill. Instead, Bill turned out to be dark haired, about half a head taller than me, with dark brown eyes, and five o'clock shadow I guessed had arrived around noon. He was wearing a red, buttoned shirt, open at the collar, which revealed dark chest hairs at his throat.

He was freaking hot. I felt myself blushing when their kiss continued for longer than was polite. Eventually, Johnny slid free from Bill's hands.

"Bill, this is Cam. Cam, this is Bill."

Bill smiled at me, and I kept my hands in my front pockets,

even though it gave me a "bumpkin" look. I didn't shake hands, for obvious reasons.

"Nice to meet you," I said.

"Come on in," he said.

We went inside, where another man was sitting on the couch. Tate, I assumed. He, too, was dark haired—though his hair was very short—and he had a tan that bordered on sunburn. He was wearing a white T-shirt, which was snug against his thick chest and broad shoulders, and faded jeans. He rose as we walked in and grinned at me.

"This is the psychic?" Tate had a deep voice.

I froze and turned what I hoped was a withering look at Johnny, who mostly ignored it and shrugged at me.

Fantastic. Now I had a whole evening ahead of me of being the freak. I was going to kill Johnny.

I settled on nodding, and then—*fuck it*—said, "Yeah."

Bill let out a kind of snort. Oh, this was going to be fun.

"Who's hungry?" Johnny chirped.

Johnny sat across from me, Bill to my left, and Tate to my right. The steaks were great, and though I tried to find a way to casually brush against Tate or Bill, the opportunity hadn't really presented itself, and besides that...

Besides that, there was *something* about them. Bill's aura would flash with yellow amusement just before Tate would tell a joke, and when Bill groped Johnny (which he seemed to do a lot), Tate's aura flushed with the royal purple I'd long learned to associate with being turned on. I couldn't decide if they were teasing each other or enjoying the interplay.

Dinner conversation was lively, Tate telling many stories of people and events that obviously delighted Bill and left Johnny growing more annoyed as the meal passed. I sat back, watching, trying to make sense of the brief flashes I got. I saw glimpses of places when Tate would mention somewhere and Bill would know it, and picked up faces when they discussed people they knew. The most interesting thing, however, was what seemed to be a kind of thread not-quite-strung between Bill and Tate. Not a silver cord, I'd seen that before, between my mother and my stepfather. I held seeing a silver cord as the standard of true love, but this was...shimmery, and though it seemed to reach out from one man to the other, it didn't connect. I couldn't figure it out, and it was hard to catch—I saw it mostly out of the corner of my eye and couldn't pin down any color.

When we were done, Tate rose, grabbing his plate. I started to rise as well, figuring to help, but Tate said, "No, I got it—" and I said "Oh, sorry—" and our fingers collided against my plate.

"Holy shit," I said, sitting down hard and grabbing at the side of my stomach as the images—and the sensation—struck me. "You got *shot*?"

Tate held the plates, looking at me, then slowly glanced at Bill, and then turned to Johnny.

"That's not fucking funny," he said, his voice angry.

"What?" Johnny frowned, looking at Tate, then Bill, then me. "Is he right? Did you get shot?" Johnny's eyebrows were high. "When did you get shot?"

"Two years ago," Bill said to Johnny, then, looking back at Tate, he added evenly, "I didn't tell him. I swear."

"Sorry," I said, still a bit shaken from the vision. Tate turned his angry glare back on me. His jaw was set, and his brown eyes were cold. The image of blood-stained hands slammed into my head so vibrantly I had to blink to dismiss it.

"How did you know? Did you fucking Google me?" Tate was yelling.

I shook my head, getting angry myself. "No, you *asshole*, I didn't Google you. Johnny told you, I'm psychic."

"Bullshit," Tate snapped.

"Fine," I said, and rose. "I'm not psychic. I can't tell that you're totally turned on every time Bill grabs Johnny's dick. And I can't possibly know that Bill does it on purpose, because he knows it gets you going. I didn't feel the bullet go in here "—I pointed at my stomach, on the left side—"or come out here. Or that your hands were covered with your blood. I'll leave. I'm sorry to have bothered you; I never should have come in the first place." I felt tears in my eyes. There was no way I was going to let them see *that*. Johnny rose, mouth agape, but didn't try to stop me. I headed for the door.

"Wait," Johnny said, but it was halfhearted at best, and I left, slamming the door behind me.

"We broke up," Johnny said, slumping into the chair across from me.

I sighed and put my coffee down. I hadn't heard him approach, and I had chosen a table at the back of the coffee shop in hopes of not seeing him. It was a quiet Sunday, though, and he'd found me.

"That's too bad," I said. I was still pissed he'd told them about me being psychic.

Johnny sat down across from me. "You know what happened after you left?"

I eyed him. Did it look like I wanted to know?

"Tate went to his room to sulk," Johnny said, though I had a hard time imagining a guy as tough as Tate *sulking*. "And Bill started accusing me of setting it all up."

I winced, feeling a little bad. "Sorry."

"We've fought before," Johnny said lightly, waving his hand.

"By the time we went to bed, he was all over me again, and fucked me blind."

I winced again, feeling a lot less bad.

"But then, *right after he gets off*, he starts in on it again, asking me if I'd set that all up, or if you really were psychic." Johnny rolled his eyes. "I'd told him the story of how you saw that car crash about a hundred times, but he thought you were full of shit."

I shrugged. I was used to that.

"So I said, 'Well, Bill, you tell me. Do you really grab me just so that Tate can watch?'" Johnny opened his eyes wide. "You know what he said?"

I shrugged.

"He said, 'Yeah.'" Johnny shivered. "'Yeah, I do.' Then he starts confessing that—if I'd *like* to—he thinks it'd be pretty hot if he could fuck me in front of Tate, and maybe I could suck Tate off, too, if I'd like that."

I felt myself blushing. To be honest, that didn't sound as disgusting as Johnny was making it out to be. Playing piggy in the middle with Tate and Bill? Gosh, that'd be just awful, wouldn't it? Absolutely. Real torture.

"So I told him to go fuck himself, grabbed my clothes and took off."

I blinked.

Johnny sighed. "I know. He had his flaws, but...what a cock!" He shrugged. "Still, I mean...I'm not into the whole threesome thing." I flashed on Johnny, in his apartment, on his bed just staring at the ceiling. It surprised me. Johnny's feelings were really hurt, but he wasn't upset so much as he was pissed off. Suddenly, it hit me. Johnny loved being the center of attention. Bill's request offended his sense of self-worth. Why would anyone want *more* than Johnny?

I couldn't help it, I smiled.

Johnny nodded, misinterpreting. "Seriously. What a cock." He shrugged. "Whatever. Moving on. This, uh...is why I need the favor."

I leaned back. "Favor?"

"If I gave you my key, would you go in on Monday night and get my stuff? They'll be at the game. It's not a lot of stuff, but I think I left my cell phone, my Aveda stuff, and a couple of my shirts—especially the black one that makes me look hot."

I held up my hand. "And you can't because...?"

"Well..." Johnny had the grace to blush. "I have a date."

I shook my head. "Don't tell me. Big blond, tattoo on the back of his left shoulder?"

"Seriously?" He was delighted. "Glen has a tattoo?"

I sighed. "He also has black silk sheets."

"Really?" Johnny wrinkled his nose. "Well, everyone has a flaw. Here are my keys."

He slid them across the table.

Monday night, I found myself outside their condo, waiting until I saw them get into Bill's jeep and pull out of the lot. I sighed, fished out Johnny's keys and let myself into the building.

Once inside, I shrugged off my backpack and looked around, remembering Johnny's list. I started in the bathroom, finding his hair gunk and toothbrush, and was just stepping back out into the main room when I heard the front door.

"...Forgot to lock it," Bill said, and stepped inside, Tate behind him.

Both froze when they saw me.

"What are you doing here?" Bill said.

I held up Johnny's keys. "Johnny...uh, asked me to get his stuff..."

Tate was staring at me, but Bill was the one to speak again. "He sent you?"

I nodded. Clashing images were running through my head—Tate angry, Bill shaking his head—had they actually fought? I couldn't make sense of it all, and amid all that, there was the strange not-quite-there of the threads that didn't quite go anywhere, but attached to the two men. I rubbed my eyes.

"So...he's done," Bill said, and though there was some sadness in his voice, I got no sense of grief. He was a little sad, but not devastated. More like a little let down, but not surprised.

"He doesn't get how close you guys are," I found myself saying. That made Bill pause, and his eyes met mine. I looked down. The man had an intense gaze.

Tate spoke. "How did you know about me getting shot?"

I took a breath, but he didn't seem angry. "I see things. Not on purpose, and usually when I touch people. It's not... It can be..." I paused, holding the hair gel and toothbrush awkwardly. "It is what it is. Weren't you going to a hockey game?"

"Bill forgot the tickets," Tate said.

"I told you to bring them," Bill said.

I couldn't help it, I smiled. They looked at each other a moment, then Bill walked past me and stepped into the furthest bedroom.

Tate regarded me. "Johnny's really gone, huh?"

I nodded. "He's a bit too self-centered to...uh..." I wasn't sure how to put it.

"He told you what Bill asked?"

"Yeah." I shrugged, face reddening. "Like I said, he doesn't get how close you guys are." I thought of the strange thread that did—but didn't—connect them.

Tate regarded me, an odd look on his face.

"Got 'em," Bill said, coming back into the room.

"You like hockey?" Tate asked me. He was wearing the red jersey of the home team, as was Bill.

"Yeah," I said.

"We have an extra ticket," he said. Bill glanced at him, surprised.

"I'm not good with crowds," I said, apologetic.

"We got a box," Bill said, looking at me after a moment.

I had a flash, seeing a board and numbers. "They're going to massacre the Leafs tonight, six to three."

Bill raised an eyebrow, but Tate actually smiled. It surprised me.

"Okay. I'm game," he said. "There's no way you could Google that. Come on. Let's go see." He slapped Bill on the shoulder. "I'll even apologize if they do."

We went.

We came back hours later, laughing. Our team had indeed taken the game, 6-3, and all the way home, Tate kept repeating, "I can't fucking believe it," and turning to look at me, but not like I was a freak. Bill drove mostly silent, occasionally asking questions, which I tried to answer honestly, and the two of them listened to my answers without scoffing. When we got back to the condo, it suddenly occurred to me that I hadn't gotten the rest of Johnny's stuff. I picked up my backpack.

"He wants his shirts, and his cell phone, too."

They helped me gather Johnny's stuff. A few minutes later, the three of us were standing in the entranceway. I found myself more than a little sad that the evening was ending, and more aware than ever how masculine and handsome the two men were. I turned to Tate, who was giving me a crooked smile, and with a mental *fuck it!* I rolled forward on my toes, put my hands against his chest and gave him a kiss.

He grunted in surprise, but kissed me back, tongue quickly in my mouth, and his hands taking my shoulders.

"Happy Birthday," I said, rocking back. A pulse of deep purple—lust—flashed before my eyes.

He grinned at me, dark eyes glinting.

I let my hands slowly slide down his chest, which was hard and warm through his jersey, until my right hand stopped on the edge of his stomach, near his left side.

"Right here, right?"

He nodded.

I leaned back slightly, about to step away, and my shoulders bumped into Bill, who I realized was tight behind me.

Deep purple again.

"You know what I'd really like to get him for his birthday?" Bill asked, voice low. I pressed against him a little and felt the hardness of his dick against my back. My eyes met Tate's, and I saw him flick his gaze over my shoulder, at Bill.

I blinked and saw myself on my hands and knees between them. Oh, my. I took a shaky breath.

"I think so," I said, and let my right hand slide farther down Tate's body, turning my fingers down until I cupped his crotch through his jeans. I felt him stiffen. I moved my left hand behind me, sliding it between my back and Bill till I was cupping his crotch the same way.

"You *are* psychic," Bill said, amusement in his voice.

"Told you," I said, and shifted up to kiss Tate again. This time one of his hands took the back of my head and he kissed me possessively, his tongue intruding. Bill pressed harder against my back, pushing me into Tate, and wrapped his arms around us both. I tilted my head, letting Tate's tongue go, and Bill leaned around and kissed me, his stubble rough on my chin and cheek.

I started to fumble with Tate's belt, and Tate laughed, which broke us all up long enough to start the stumbling walk toward the closest bedroom—Tate's?—unbuttoning and kicking off shoes as I alternately kissed Bill and Tate, and tugged at their jerseys and belts.

Bill's chest was hairy, Tate's less so, though he had a patch that led down to the waistband of his boxers. Both had developed chests and thick arms. The feel of kissing Tate while Bill's hairy chest pressed against my back had me spinning, and Tate's hands teased my nipples, pinching lightly while Bill's stubble scraped against my neck with his kisses.

It was sensory overload, even without the images flashing through my mind.

We broke through the door and Tate flicked on the light as he walked backward to the bed, tugging me along by the waist of my jeans, Bill directly behind me. When the back of his legs hit the bed, he took a moment to shuck his jeans completely, and I tugged his boxers down with a jerk, freeing his long, slightly curved cock.

He sat on the bed, then slid himself back, legs spread, until he reached the headboard. His dick rose, and I saw the puckered scar on the left side of his stomach.

Bill released me, and I crawled onto the bed, ignoring Tate's dick just long enough to give one quick kiss and lick to the scar. Tate laughed, then grabbed my head with both hands, turning my face up to look at him.

"Nice," he said.

I pushed free and swallowed his dick as deeply as I could in one hot swallow.

"Nicer!" Tate breathed.

The bed shifted, and I realized that Bill had joined us. Soon I felt him tugging at my jeans, and I had to brace myself on my hands for a moment, letting Tate's cock slip from my mouth while Bill got my jeans and then my briefs off. My own uncut cock was unsheathed and hard.

Bill's hands massaged my asscheeks.

"Sweet," he said, and as I put Tate's cock back into my mouth, I felt Bill's hot tongue and rough stubble at my ass. I moaned into Tate's dick, and squirmed my ass against Bill's mouth. Images burst through my mind: Bill fucking me. Me in handcuffs. Waving good-bye as Bill drove off, while Tate's arm was around my shoulder. Tate fucking me. Welcoming Bill back with steaks, and a kiss. Bill sucking me while Tate held me from behind, twisting my nipples. Being blindfolded. Sucking one of them, both of them, taking both of their dicks deep inside my ass at the same time. The images were fast, barely glimpses, but I had to hold still for a moment, braced between Bill's tongue and Tate's upward thrusts to stop myself from coming on the spot. The images faded, and I went back to work, trying to take the full length of Tate's hardness into my mouth and moving one hand up his hard chest, rolling one nipple between my finger and thumb.

His hands curled in my hair. "Yeah," he said. "Suck it..."

Bill's tongue assaulted my ass, and I was moaning around Tate's dick. After a few more exquisite moments, Bill's tonguing stopped, and I felt one of his fingers tease my hole. I pushed back against him and heard him laugh.

"You want to get fucked, Cam?" he asked.

My answer was an extended moan around Tate's thickness and an urgent shove of my ass against Bill's finger, pushing it deeper into me. He chuckled, then removed his finger. I felt the bed move as he got up, and I heard his belt jingle as he stripped off his jeans and underwear. He walked to the side of the bed—I could see the man's hairy thighs as he opened the drawer beside where I was sucking Tate and pulled something out. When he was on the bed again, the sudden cool slickness of lube poured between my asscheeks, and Bill's finger rubbed it in and around my hole.

Tate's dick slipped from my mouth as I arched my head back and said, "Fuck..."

"Hey, now," Tate said quietly. He met my gaze. "Suck," he said.

Bill gripped my waist and tugged me back up onto my knees. I heard the sound of a condom package tearing open, and after what felt like ages, Bill's finger returned.

I sucked, desperately pressing back against Bill's finger, which seemed to do nothing but tease. Just when I was about to let Tate's cock out of my mouth again to beg Bill to put his cock in me, I felt hot tip of his cock against my hole. A guttural moan escaped from me, the whole of it translating down Tate's cock. He groaned and swore, and I sucked and slurped and ran my tongue in circles around the tip of his dick, bobbing my head up and down the length of him as fast as I could.

Bill entered me with agonizing slowness. I pushed back against him, though the strong man easily held me back, controlling his depth. I heard him breathing out deeply as his cock slid into me, inch after veined inch, and I heard Johnny's voice: *What a cock!* Bill was thick and filled me with a heat I could barely stand.

I sucked Tate wildly now, feeling his dark pubic hair against my lips, having swallowed the full length of him. He groaned, cursed and gasped as I sucked, and when Bill's balls hit the back of my ass, I thought he might split me. I was moaning around Tate's dick when Bill pulled his length nearly all the way out, and then pushed back in again, faster than his first stroke.

"Fuck, that's hot," Tate said. My eyes were watering from holding him in my mouth. I worked my lips around the base of his cock and felt it at the back of my throat.

Bill picked up his pace quickly, riding my ass roughly, hands gripping my waist even as I felt my sweat making his grip slick. His own sweat hit my back as he slammed into me, and I felt Tate's hands twist and grip in my hair. My cock was rock hard.

"Fuck!" Tate's body jerked up against my face, and I felt his cock spasm as his load burst. He filled my mouth with cum, hot and salty. I tried to swallow, but missed most of it. I felt it pour out of my mouth around the shaft of his cock and into his pubic hair. He jerked again, and a second blast filled my mouth, one I managed to swallow. Then his cock slid free, and he rubbed my face in the spunk in his crotch.

Bill pushed deep into me, and after hearing him give a bellow of his own, I felt his hot load surge once, twice, and then three times with thick spasms. My back curled, my face pressed against Tate's thigh.

He grunted, then fell against me, and I half rolled, my face pressed against Tate's side, and Bill on top of me, pulling his dick free with one hand. I gripped my dick in my right hand and stroked barely a half-dozen times before I felt my own orgasm sending hot wads of cum onto Tate's left leg and stomach.

We lay there panting for some time. I closed my eyes, and then when I opened them, something was very different.

A silver cord, shining and bright, spun from Tate's stomach and into mine. When I glanced down at it in wonder, I saw that from my own stomach, the thread split and passed through me. I craned my neck just enough to see it threaded into Bill's hairy abdomen.

I was stunned. That was...that meant... "Holy fuck."

"Damn straight," Bill laughed, and slapped my ass. He got up, and came back with a wet towel, wiping my face, and Tate's crotch and leg and stomach. He'd disposed of the condom. As

Bill moved around, I looked at Tate, who was stretched out on the bed, his eyes half-lidded, cock still semihard and a sly grin on his face. He looked at me, and a burst of silver light flared down the link between us, and I felt it pass through me, and move on to Bill, who lay back down on the bed.

"You gotta try that." Tate spoke over my head. "Cam's a born cocksucker." I laughed out loud.

"Give me a minute to catch my breath," Bill said, and I looked at him. He winked.

"Sure," I said. "Maybe you can get those handcuffs."

"Johnny told you about the handcuffs?" Bill asked, surprised.

"No." I shook my head. "Psychic, remember? I see things." I turned and looked at him, arranging myself on my back between them. With a hand on each cock, I started to stroke them. Tate let out a low grumbling moan, and Bill sighed.

"Things?" Tate said, closing his eyes.

"Things," I said. "You ship out soon, Bill, so we shouldn't waste time getting to the other stuff." My hands worked them.

"What else"—Bill's breath hitched—"did you see?"

"Well, for starters…" I took him into my mouth.

And showed them both.

SEXATHON

Rachel Kramer Bussel

When Doug told me he wanted to enter the sexathon at
our local sex club, at first, I looked at him like he was
crazy. We've been together for ten years, and in many ways it
seems like a lifetime. I'm thirty-five and he's twenty-nine and
most of our friends are only now starting to talk weddings and
babies. They look to us as a model couple, and maybe we are. I
often joke that we're like any old married couple—we tied the
knot four years ago, finally—with each of us having our own
spot on the couch, our pillow, our mug; in short, our places
within our home. Yet we both welcome those niceties, those
symbols that go far beyond the solid gold wedding rings we
exchanged during the ceremony. And we'd been monogamous,
save for a few random threesomes we'd taken part in, which had
been hot—don't get me wrong—but in general we were one-
man men, focused on building our lives together, eager to share
everything from sex to breakfast to road trips. The adventures
we'd shared up until then, including traveling everywhere from

Belize to Alaska, as well as being godparents to our friends' son
Peter, had only brought us closer together. We had our spats,
sure, but I was certain that without Doug my life would be far
worse off than the one we shared.

Doug explained that the club was having a fundraiser, but
instead of a marathon or walkathon, it was a sexathon. You got
points for everything from deep-throating a dildo to how far
you ejaculated when you jerked off to how many partners you
hooked up with, and people were supposed to pledge a dollar
or more for every point you earned. Condoms would be manda-
tory. When he told me about the points and prizes—a trip to
Paris, a big-screen plasma TV—I knew there was no talking him
out of it. The thing about my man, though you'd never know it
unless you were in a specifically sporting situation with him, is
that he's incredibly competitive. Whether it's doing crossword
puzzles, guessing the answers on *Jeopardy,* playing bingo at our
gay community center or even taking part in pickup softball, he
plays to win.

"What about me?" I asked. I'm not insecure, but even the
most solid long-term relationship can hit its rough spots. Was he
having a midlife crisis? Did he regret not having more partners in
his younger years? We'd discussed this, and not just when we first
got together. Back then, we'd been youthful and idealistic, and
while we were definitely falling in love with each other in those
days, we were also in love with the idea of love. I thought the men
who picked up a different trick every night were fools. Who'd
want a new cock when you could have a man like Doug: tall,
strapping, husky, hairy; who could be by turns savage (teeth and
nails clawing at me), and tender (taking care of me in countless
ways)? Not me. And those kisses! The kind that went on forever,
that left me breathless, that seemed to come out of nowhere and
for no reason—he'd stop me in the middle of a sentence just for

the pleasure of sticking his tongue down my throat.

Yet over the years we've each wondered, occasionally aloud, what else is out there? Who might we have missed by our focus on each other? So on one level, I understood; this wasn't just about his cocksmanship or pride, but something deeper. Was he trying to test the waters? Was he looking for a fling or a new husband? I had so many questions, but my most vulnerable one was what I wound up speaking aloud, three little words that betrayed my nervousness.

"Baby," he said, pulling me close till our foreheads were touching, "I love you. I always will. This is just something I feel I need to do. I'll be safe, you know that, and you can come watch and cheer me on."

I thought it over for the rest of the day, but something about that scenario didn't sit well with me. I'm not exactly like Doug, which is what has made us so compatible in the long term. I'm more laid-back, whereas he's, if not high-strung, certainly excitable. I care less about winning than about doing things I enjoy; I'll get so involved in a crossword puzzle clue that I'll go research one of the answers and even read a book about the topic. I'm a detail man whereas Doug is about the big picture. But for all that, I knew immediately what I was going to do: I would enter that sexathon right alongside Doug—and hopefully win and raise even more money than him.

I came to him that night as he was reading a murder mystery. "I have something to tell you," I said quietly, as I took the paperback from his hands and curled up facing him.

"You're really pissed, huh?" he asked.

"No, not really. But I'm not just going to be there cheering you on. I'm going to be entering the competition too."

"You?" he asked, squinting at me, clearly surprised.

"What do you mean? Don't think I have what it takes?"

Maybe he meant that since I'm a bottom, with him, anyway, almost all of the time—it wasn't always like that with other lovers—that I was somehow not as qualified. Or maybe he just didn't think of me like that; I was the one who'd rather watch everyone else climb a mountain than sweat it out myself.

"Of course, I just...I'm surprised. But I can't wait to watch you compete," he said with a grin, before tackling me, his cock already hard. I sank into the sheer pleasure of being with the man I loved, grateful he wasn't upset, and more than a little excited about the prospect of taking on new lovers and a new adventure.

This wasn't the kind of event we trained for. We fucked, certainly, but we'd always done plenty of that. Our sex was good: frenzied at times, slow at others. But we didn't go out of our way to try anything new or introduce any new toys or tricks into the bedroom. And we didn't say another word to each other about the sexathon; instead, we each hit up our mutual friends, along with select coworkers and other trusted acquaintances. We didn't share how much was pledged, though that would be posted on the wall at the event.

Time flew, and soon we were as ready as we'd ever be. Though we'd be naked for most of the event, we got to pick our starting outfits. Doug decided to wear a pair of snug new black-and-white-striped briefs that did a lot to emphasize his already generous package. He wore jeans and a T-shirt over the briefs, but once we arrived, he stowed those away. I went the opposite route, showing up in my favorite soft gray pants and an elegant, crisp white button-down shirt, my hair freshly combed, two days' worth of stubble on my chin. No underwear.

Our friend Al greeted us when we came in. "Well, well, well. You two are quite the catch. And the only couple who's signed up."

"Well, we're not a team today," said Doug. "It's every man for himself. Right, baby?" He grabbed my ass and gave me a kiss. It was a powerful kiss, but I could sense the tension thrumming through him, the uncertainty over what, exactly, was going to happen in the next few hours. I kissed him back and tried to reassure him with my lips. No matter what, he was the only man for me.

We were each given a number and told to report for duty. There were eight tasks, and we'd be graded on all of them. They were: deep-throating a dildo, rolling an extra-large condom onto an extra-large real cock, getting spanked, boot worshipping, coming as far as you could, getting a butt plug up someone's ass, bobbing for cocks (think bobbing for apples). The final stage: all the contestants would be put in a giant room and have to compete to have as many partners as they could in an hour (multiple partners permitted, up to four).

This would be quite the test; some of the men, judging from a quick glance around, were hot, but some weren't my type. Many were wiry and thin, while I prefer, if not bears, more meaty guys. I had to remind myself that it wasn't about being attracted to them necessarily, but simply going for it, doing things I'd never have done in any other circumstance. I'm not shy by any means, but pre-Doug, I'd always wanted to at least know the guy's name. Here the men were just numbers; myself included (I was seven while Doug was eight). There were twenty contestants and probably double that number cheering us, while various guys volunteered their services, as it were.

I felt pumped up with adrenaline, and in a weird way, even though we'd be competing against each other, it made me feel close to Doug. I'd never have done anything like this without him, and now I was inspired by his team spirit, or rather, sex spirit. It made me want to let him tie me up, as he's always begged to do, and have his way with me fully, completely. But first, there was a sexathon to win.

There were some tasks I knew I'd be great at, and some that I'd never contemplated, let alone tried. First up was deep-throating. I do pride myself on being able to take all of Doug's wide nine-inch cock down my throat, so I figured this would be an easy task. But it's one thing to get down on my knees and sword swallow my best friend and husband, quite another to have my hands tied behind my back and have to open wide for a piece of silicone that smelled nothing like a human cock. Lined up next to me were nine other men, including Doug. Part of me was tempted to peek at him, but I knew that would throw me off track—others had the same idea because I did glimpse a blindfold or two—so I shut my eyes and, when I heard the bell go off, opened wide and started sucking. The dicks weren't being rammed down our throats, but were held in place by a man who'd be judging us on technique, attention to balls, saliva control and so on. At first, I almost spit out the dick, but then I harkened back to my college theater roots and simply pretended the cock was Doug's.

Then it was easy: I lavished attention on the head, pretending its owner was patting my hair, moaning and praising me, then started to slide my wet lips along the length of the toy. I'd actually given head to toys before, prior to their going up my ass, and the more I did it, the more into it I got. The room was filled with slurping and sucking sounds and the occasional grunt or sigh or exclamation. I was quiet, studious almost; I usually let Doug make the noise when I'm sucking him off. Before I knew it, a bell went off. We'd find out how we'd done later. My jaw was a bit sore, but it had been fun—though not as fun as getting a mouthful of Doug's cream on my tongue.

Next up was condom-rolling. I figured this was the easiest

task, except that Doug and I had been fluid bonded for so long and save for those threesomes, hadn't had to use condoms. I figured it would come back to me, like riding a bike, but it didn't quite work out that way. The condom was slippery, and we only had one minute total; the first three to complete the task got bonus points. They'd switched things up from the first round—instead of the rubber going on a fake cock, we got the real thing. I was putting a condom on a stranger, and I couldn't help but blush. His dick was big and thick and the sight of it was entrancing. I didn't dare look up at him as I held the base in one hand. First I started rolling the condom down the wrong way, then I had to quickly shift gears. I got his cock covered just before the buzzer went off.

Then we were led into a room with ten padded spanking benches and instructed to bend over and hold on to our ankles. "You will be spanked with a hand, a ruler, a paddle and a belt. You may use the safeword *pussy* at any time, but points will be deducted for that. All our tops have been trained to provide the same amount of sensation, for twenty lashes each. Are you ready?"

We murmured our agreement. I wasn't just ready; I was extremely hard. I love getting spanked, and the novelty of having someone new spank me was arousing. My competitive streak kicked in, because I knew that this round would be a challenge for Doug. He's 100 percent top; he just doesn't have a submissive bone—let alone boner—in his body. I held on and got ready. A hand covered my right asscheek, then when the whistle blew, it began to smack me methodically: right, left, right, left. I got used to the rhythm of the smacks and was eager for the ruler when it started. The man hitting me used the ruler to strike both cheeks at once. A few times, I clenched my bottom and he rapped it against me to get me to unclench and be fully in the spirit of what we were doing. "Give me that ass," the man whispered in my ear, and for some reason, I wanted to. I shuddered as his words traveled through my body and I relaxed into the bench so he could properly pound me. The whacks were stronger, making my skin tingle. I was grateful we didn't have to count out loud because there was so much noise in the room, it was easy to lose track. I preferred to savor each wave of heat coursing through my bottom, sending pleasure right through to my dick.

I was fine with the ruler and paddle, but the belt was a lot for me to handle. I focused on taking deep breaths and again, thought of Doug, not whimpering in pain, but praising me after I'd lain across his lap and taken my blows like a good boy. Despite my resolve, a few tears managed to escape my eyes and travel down my neck. The man gently wiped them away when he was done and offered me the belt to kiss. It was an oddly tender moment as slaps rang out across the room.

Then it was time for boot worship, and again, my oral prowess came in handy. I love using my tongue—or having it used—and I was so consumed by the feel, smell and taste of the leather and I forgot to look for Doug among the others. I got lost in the sensation, hoping, in those minutes, only that the recipient of my tongue-lashing enjoyed it. From the groans he was making, I was pretty sure he did.

Then we got a bit of a break in the form of masturbation. Doug and I stood next to each other, and in this case, it helped me. Our goal was to shoot as far across the room as we could, something I'd practiced out the window of my college dorm late at night, so I was pretty good at it. Nothing so far had involved my cock, save for getting spanked, and I was ready. I'd deliberately pulled back from Doug that morning when he'd wanted to fuck me for good luck. He has a faster recovery time than I do, and I didn't want to jinx things. I snuck glances at him as I worked myself, then at the other men, realizing that regardless of who won, it was a treat to be in a room with nineteen other men beating their meat. I figured my advantage would be in holding off as long as possible to see where the competition landed. As it turned out, watching stream after stream of come erupt from men's cocks is extremely exciting! I managed to wait until it was just me and Doug, and I was so horny I couldn't stand it, and I let loose, almost spraying a guy who apparently didn't think I could make it all the way across the room—or maybe he did and he wanted some. "Oh, Matt," Doug said, watching me and then shooting a lot of come, but pretty much right in front of him. Despite his showing, there was a huge smile on Doug's face when he was done.

Next were the butt plugs, and we were given a bucket from which to choose: slim or fat, black or red or silver or purple; there were all shapes and sizes. I chose a red one with three ridges, since part of what we'd be judged on was how much pleasure we brought our partner, along with size, amount of lube, speed and accuracy. We were all paired with guys who loved getting fucked, and though I didn't know the man's name, his beautiful olive-skinned asshole spoke to me. He was on the ground, on his knees, his hands reaching behind to hold that sweet hole open just for me. I added some lube to my thumb while around us the judges took notes.

I'd only done Doug back there a few times, because he's not that into it but occasionally let me because I like it. Here I couldn't really engage in an extended dialogue with the guy, so I had to go by his body language, and from the way he was pressing back against me, I knew he wanted me to get going with the toy. I withdrew my thumb, slightly reluctantly, and then heard Doug's voice coaxing his bottom to let him in.

"Oh, yeah, you dirty boy, give it to me, you slut," he said. For a second, I was jealous, but then I remembered the words he'd used that morning to try to coax me into bed. "You're going to be punished for teasing me, Matt." Oh, I hoped I would be. I hoped that any jealousy this event incited would serve to bring us closer together, because the truth was I'd have left butt plug guy there waiting if Doug had approached me right then. I looked at him for a few more seconds before returning to the task at hand.

The plug was easily swallowed by the man's hungry anus, which sucked it right in. I teased him by twirling it around and pulling it out, only to slowly shove it back in, making sure he felt every ridge of the toy. When time was called, twenty male asses were faceup, on display, all but one stuffed with a plug; the guy who'd missed had apparently chosen a toy that was too big for its intended recipient.

Then, I got to stick my face in what felt like a sea of cocks. There was no water, but there were men crowded together, their hard dicks bobbing and weaving as they jerked them slowly, while I tried to capture one in my mouth. We'd each be given this chance, so the men were instructed not to come. It was exciting to feel so many penises within reach of my tongue; at one point I just trailed the tip of my tongue along the heads before finding one I wanted, and I guess my lips felt good enough that he forgot he was supposed to be evading me. I swallowed all of it, then rose and teased the head, feeling his body jerk until he pulled it out and slapped it against my face. Then my time was up.

We were ushered into the waiting area where there were light snacks and sodas. I smiled at another contestant. "How's it going?" I asked.

"Great, man, just great. I've been having a dry spell so when I heard about this I signed right up. But you two—wow! I don't know if I'd have the courage to do what you're doing."

I pondered what he'd said. I hadn't thought of it as courage per se, but it was a sign of us having faith that our relationship wouldn't be derailed by a little extracurricular fun. I knew that at that moment, the only man I really wanted to fuck was Doug, my familiar, sexy, tough, gorgeous Doug. He walked into the room and came right over to me. "You were amazing out there," he said, like I'd been race-car driving or something.

"You watched me?" I asked.

"Of course; I couldn't get enough. And now I'm going to watch men fuck you."

"What about you?" I asked.

"You know what? I realized that I'd really rather watch. There were a few hotties, but only one I want like that," he said and pulled me close for a kiss. After our tongues had gotten reacquainted, I pulled back.

"Do you mean you want me to drop out too and are just being polite?"

"Not at all, babe. You go get 'em, just save a little something for me." At that moment, my heart, not to mention my cock, swelled. Doug was not only the sexiest guy I'd ever known, he was going above and behind. He wanted to see me take the gold, and I'd be damned if I wasn't going to make him proud!

The room was filled with men in tight red spandex shorts, who would be our pool of partners; we could also add on other contestants but then we'd each get points. Hand jobs got you one point, blow jobs two, rimming three, fucking four. We had twenty minutes. I strolled in totally nude and immediately set eyes on a guy about ten years older than me, though I only surmised that from his white hair. Otherwise he was strong, his muscles showing through. I eyed him up and down and he peeled down his shorts to show me the impressive cock waiting for me. I turned back to look at Doug on the sidelines and he gave me a thumbs-up.

I grabbed the man's cock and while I did, reached for a kid who had to be just over the twenty-one-year-old cutoff. I snapped his shorts and he turned, looking for a moment like he didn't know how he'd gotten there. The truth was, neither did I, but I wanted them both. I pulled him over to me and soon I was sandwiched between them. "Let me fuck you while you rim him," the older man whispered in my ear. I'd never done two guys at once, but I was game. The boy got on his stomach and spread his legs and I didn't stop to think, just lunged for his balls with my tongue while the other man lubed me up, and then I felt his condom-covered cock pushing into me. Soon his cock was inside me, his thrusts shoving my face into the young guy's ass, while around me the smells and sounds of sex filled the air. It was hot, for sure, but my cock was hard for one man only. "I'm gonna come," I heard the older guy say, and I braced myself for his jizz.

When he was done, and the younger one still showed no signs of coming, I flipped junior over and jerked him off while pressing two lubed-up fingers up his ass. That did the trick, and he gave us all a delightful treat as he came all over his chest. I had already found my next partners, two men who looked achingly alike, who were holding hands. "I want to jerk you both off," I said. "Over there," I added, pointing to where Doug was sitting.

They obliged, and I found that in this context, I liked being in control, rubbing their dicks together, making one get on top of the other when my hands were tired, then blowing both of them. Doug clapped softly next to me. The rest of the free-for-all was a blur of hands and tongues and cocks and toys. I wound up wearing nipple clamps and sporting a giant erection. When the buzzer sounded, I raced over to Doug, who held out one of our soft, plush towels from home for me then carefully took off the clamps, while the judges told us they had to calculate. "Your time is your own until we're ready."

"You're gonna win," Doug said, to which I replied, "I don't care."

"Well, I do. I want to show you off next time we come here, parade you around with your winning medal on your chest—or your cock." He laughed, and so did I, and then his hand was on my cock and I couldn't think about anything else but the way he was touching me. It was the same as hundreds, maybe even thousands, of other hand jobs he'd given me, yet it felt different, more special for us having gone through a sexual marathon (mostly) together. Fittingly, I was coating his hand with my cream when they came in to announce the winners. When my name was called, I burst out with a cry of excitement, then leapt up to collect the gold cock statue and, yes, a medal. I couldn't wear it on my flaccid cock just then, but I looked forward to hanging it above our bed—and trying new things with Doug whenever one of us got the urge.

"Speech! Speech!" the guys filling the room cried out.

"Okay, okay," I conceded, standing and putting my arm around Doug. "I wouldn't be here if it weren't for the love of my life, Doug, who is the best husband a guy could ask for. Maybe next year there should be a doubles category, like in tennis, because I don't want to even think about trying to fuck anyone without him." The applause was deafening, almost—I still heard Doug when he whispered, "I love you," in my ear.

SANDWICH ARTIST

Shane Allison

I stole the keys out of Ma's purse. It was a damn shame that I was still living at home. My sister got out early at the sweet age of eighteen. She couldn't take the curfews and the beatings that came if she was a minute late. I never could get it right. I should have left for New York as soon as I finished junior college. Yet, had I done that, I never would have met Armando. I waited until they'd gone to bed, fighting off fears in their nightmares. The road I live on was slick with mud, the holes overrun with rainwater from last night's storm. I hate the house with its leaky roof, its cobwebbed corners and bad childhood memories. I've cried in my plate of chicken and rice, bled in the sweet ice tea. They try to keep me away from Armando with barred windows. But nothing's gonna keep me away from my baby. I put the car in NEUTRAL and pushed it with my weight out of the carport, up that slick road, through the barking of vicious pit bulls and puddles of muddy water. I'll do anything to get to him. Streetlights of white light my way through this ravenous night up Woodville Highway. I'd made it; I'd escaped the bear claws of my folks. I'd rather have run the streets like a Frenchtown whore than live with them another day. I was invisible anyway, a ghost caught in limbo between the heavens of freedom and the hell of slavery. I followed the yellow dashes that led me closer to Armando. Chris Isaac's "Wicked Game" was playing on 98.9, Armando's favorite song. I was hoarse from all the hollering. Ma had given me that *As long as you're in this house* speech. "You ain't go'n stop 'til you don' run me outta here," I yelled. "Well, go...go'n then," she screamed. So I'd be going, hauling ass and never darkening the door of Charlie Ash Lane again. They'd be sorry, those venomous bullies. Why couldn't we have been the Bradys? Why couldn't they have been Claire and Cliff Huxtable? I felt like some C-list child star. Armando and I were so close. One more paycheck and we'd have enough money to get our own place. I'd already picked out some sofas and end tables. We had our eye on this posh apartment in Verandas Villas; pricey, but nice. We'd be graduating college in three months. We were already looking for full-time jobs. We had to get away from my bible-beating parents, and his drill sergeant dad who's a staunch supporter of Don't Ask, Don't Tell.

I screeched into the lot of Jimmy John's Sandwich Shop. Armando was stocking chairs on the tables, smearing a wet mop across a linoleum floor. The moon was full and orange. Cars whooshed down the streets of South Magnolia. Armando was alone. The bell that hung above the door tolled as I walked in. The shop was redolent of sharp spices and baked breads.

"Hey, babe," I said. He stopped cleaning and walked over to give me a hug, cute in his uniform of green and black. Tufts of black hair escaped the brim of his cap. Elvis Presley sideburns ran along the sides of his face. He's a lean Italian with a skate border waistline, a body decorated with tats.

"What's wrong?" he asked.

"Nothin'," I said.

"You look mad about something." I lifted my glasses to wipe my face. "Is it your folks again?" Armando asked. "What the fuck did they do to you?" I didn't want him to worry. Armando goes off the deep end when he knows I'm upset about something. "I jus' got into anotha knock down, drag out with my mom again."

"Goddamn them," he said.

"It's no big deal," I said, taking his hand in mine.

"No, fuck that. Look, I know you love them, but your folks are assholes." My white knight and Prince Charming all rolled into one.

"Forget it. Jus' leave it alone."

"Are you hungry? Have you eaten?" Armando asked.

"Jus' a chicken biscuit from Chic-Fil-A this mornin'."

"Let me make you something. What do you want to eat?"

"I been wontuh try that new chicken Parmesan ya'll got." Armando's shirt was stained with who the hell knew what. SANDWICH ARTIST was embroidered in yellow on the top lefthand corner of his shirt. He wiped his wet hands dry on his pants.

"We gotta get you outta that house," Armando said as he yanked a pair of plastic, transparent gloves from a box next to the register. I looked at the name tag pinned to his chest.

I remembered the first time I laid eyes on Armando. It was right here at J.J.'s. I was sick of burgers and greasy Chinese food, and it was the only place open. My weight was another thing me and Ma fought about; I got sick of Ma preaching to me: "You need tuh cut back, boy." Armando had been the only one working that night when I walked in. I ordered the corned beef on wheat. I don't remember how the conversation started, but Armando and I started talking about comic books and horror movies in film history. We both agreed that *An American Werewolf in London* kicks ass. He had a beard at the time, but still looked boyish. I watched as he sprinkled my sandwich with lettuce, pickles, banana peppers. I glimpsed the sliver of a tattoo on his furred chest through the open top buttons of his uniform. I paid for my food with a twenty.

"Keep the change," I told him.

"Are you sure, man?" he asked.

"Consider it a tip." I watched him watch me, the two of us reflected in the glass door with the store's hours plastered across it. I couldn't stop thinking about him on the way home that night, with that movie-star smile, those eyes that could melt glaciers. I became a loyal customer. I tried every sandwich on the menu: from veggie to tuna and I hate fucking tuna. I would come in some nights just to see if Armando was working. Usually there was some girl with a bad dye job working, so I'd only buy lemonade or a cookie. I heard later she told him about this black dude with glasses who kept coming in and asking about him.

"All he ever bought was a cookie."

I ate a shit load of corn beef subs before I grew the balls to ask him out. After a while, I didn't want to have nothing to do with anything that ended in *sandwich*. But Armando and I grew to know each other very well.

My parents found out about Armando when Ma overheard me talking to him late one night. Life had been hell since I came out to them when I was nineteen.

"I would rather be dead than for you to be gay," she had said. I thought telling her that I was bisexual would soften the emotional blow, but she didn't care. I was going to hell either way. Daddy didn't speak to me for weeks and often referred to me as a *sissy* when he thought I couldn't hear. "Freaks," he had said. He was pissed that the family name would stop with me, his freaky, sissy son. Ma tried to get me to go to church.

"I want you to get saved like your sister." She started crying when I refused. Her preacher said that I was just running from Jesus. She stormed into my room after she so rudely eavesdropped on my conversation with Armando.

"Get off th' phone, an' come in me an' yuh daddy room." If looks could kill, hers would have skinned me alive.

"Hey, lemme call you back," I told Armando. Pearls of sweat dripped from my pits. Daddy just lay in bed with his back turned, disappointed that I was not a pussy-loving high school quarterback like he was in his heyday.

"As long azhoo in this house, I 'on' wan'choo talkin' tuh that boy."

We fussed and fought for months. I wanted to tell her to go fuck herself, but lost the nerve. Still, nothing was going to keep me away from Armando. Nothing and nobody. They put me on ten o' clock curfews, but I would always sneak out. That house was like a jail cell, a dungeon in an evil castle. If I had a dime for every scrape and scratch I'd endured to meet my Armando, I'd have enough to pay the rent on our villa apartment for the rest of the year.

I watched Armando slice the Italian herb-flavored bread.

"Did you deposit your check yet?" he asked.

"Yeah," I replied. "Did it yesterday."

"I'll be getting paid this Friday, and that oughta be enough for the security deposit and first and last months' rent." He put four pieces of breaded chicken on a sheet of wax paper and placed them in the microwave.

"We're almost there. Think I should start packing my stuff?" I asked.

"Yeah. We gotta get you from under your parents' roof. Enough's enough. If they put their hands on you again..." I'd told Armando the cuts and scratches were from my bedroom window, but I didn't think he believed me. I studied Armando's fingers as he covered one side of the bread with slices of provolone. The microwave sounded. He pulled the chicken out and onto the bread. He didn't need to ask what I wanted on the sandwich. Armando squeezed out mayo and a little mustard. Too much can ruin a sandwich. He finished it off with a decoration of green peppers, pickles and my favorite, jalapeno peppers. Armando grabbed the Parmesan, always the final ingredient, but the shaker was empty.

"I got some in back, babe," he said. My dick began to twitch in my shorts to the image of pants riding between the crack of his ass. Armando came back with the powdered cheese and a canister of fresh black olives. He knew I liked extra. He took a handful and dressed my sandwich.

"Baby, can you do me a favor?" he asked. "Could you turn the sign on the door?"

I locked the door and switched the sign to CLOSED.

"I gotta take a piss," I said, making my way to the crapper.

"I'm cleaning that one right now," he said. "Use the employee bathroom in back."

I sauntered past the big bread ovens and empty cardboard boxes. I didn't really need to go. My dick was at full salute but it wasn't because of a full bladder.

As I forked it out of my cutoff sweats, I began to think just how lucky I was to have someone as great as Armando. He's my prince. And believe me—I've had to kiss a shitload of frogs to get to him.

"Your sandwich is on the table, babe," he said, as he started to break down the boxes. I stood in the doorway watching him work while I caressed my dick, fingered my balls.

I admired him from behind as he bent and pulled cardboard. He had a black boy's ass. I cleared my throat to get his attention. I turned toward the toilet and stood in front of the mirror, fondling myself while watching a reflection of Armando's every move.

Armando moved closer to see what I was up to. He pressed the door open to get an eyeful of me working my dick.

"What are you doing?" Armando asked, grinning.

"What does it look like?" With my shorts down around my ass, and my dick thick and curved outward, I roped a hand around the back of his neck and pulled him in, giving him a warm kiss of the French persuasion. Armando's tongue tasted like pink lemonade. His lips were supple against my own. He ran his hand beneath my T-shirt, fingers traipsing through chest hair. I released a hot sigh between our bodies, as he started to jerk me off.

He paused. "Hold on," he said. "Follow me."

I tailed him around the sandwich shop, erect and anxious. Armando closed the venetians then took a chair down from one of the tables.

"Have a seat." He ran his fingers along his crotch. I couldn't wait to release that *thing* from his pants. What he doesn't have in girth, he makes up for in length. I heard Italian boys were big, and with Armando, I'll be damned if it don't ring true. He unzipped his pants and reached in to pull out his dick. The head was pink, with a shaft of muscle, veins and tender foreskin. People could see through verticals, but I was hoping the closed sign would keep voyeurs away. I took Armando's dick and tilted it up to my mouth and began to lick along the slit. I have no gag reflex, so I was able to take as much of him as I wanted down my throat.

"Look up at me," he ordered. He likes to look into my eyes while I'm sucking.

His groin was ripe with all-day crotch sweat, mixed with the scent of onions and bell peppers. I worked the head, lapping at Italian flesh.

"You know what to do," he said. I turned my attentions reluctantly from devouring his dick to sucking his balls.

"Yeah, that's it, right there." He ran his hands over my head, toying with my ears. He shaves down there, so there's no hair to get in the way. Armando lifted up his shirt, exposing that chest I adore so.

"Do it," he said. I tweaked his nipples, so sensitive under my fingers when I pull at them. My own dick was throbbing like a heart. He took off his shirt and tossed it. We didn't care where. I moved back to his dick to give him proper thanks. I was a bruised boy and he was my savior.

His legs quivered. I kneaded his flesh like dough, running my hands over his beauty-marked hips. Spit rolled along his dick as I feasted. The sandwich, wrapped tightly in paper, was within reach as well as the meat, mustard and mayo. I was hungry, but not for any sandwich.

"I got an idea." Armando looked down at me. He was annoyed I'd stopped worshipping at his altar of dick.

"Come behind here," I said, leading him by the arm, his dick wet and full. I slid my sandwich off to the side.

"Hop up," I told him, tapping the table.

"What? Why?"

"Come on, trust me," I said. The table was sturdy enough to hold Armando. He stretched his body across the cutting board easy like a cat. His socked feet stuck off one end.

"Relax." I ran one hand along a firm, hairy thigh. Armando has an awesome body, but you wouldn't know it, the way he covers up in big tees and baggy jeans, and shadows his gorgeous mug under baseball caps and hoodies. I compliment him on his body all the time, but he says he's too skinny. Armando's the only guy I know who can eat shit like pizza and burgers and never gain an ounce. Says he wants a wrestler build. He even thought of steroids at one point, but I talked him out of it.

I studied the canisters filled with lettuce, tomatoes, tufts of onions and other veggies.

"Let's see what kind of sandwich I want." I looked to the menu on the wall.

"A Cold Cut Combo." I plucked a pair of gloves out of the box and worked them over my hands. I peeled paper off slices of bologna. I spread Armando wide, and packed the cold cuts delicately between the cheeks of his tanned booty.

"Oh, it's cold," he said.

"What's next?"

"How about some pepperoni?" I patted several slices between his half moons.

"Now ham. The other white meat."

"Yeah, that'll do it," he said with growing excitement. I couldn't wait to devour this homemade man sandwich of mine. I stood back to admire my handiwork. The best part was yet to come. It was time to add color to the gustatory canvas my boyfriend had become. I thought of the dressing and was sure I wanted lettuce. I grabbed a handful and sprinkled the greenery along Armando's stuffed crevice, then added slices of juicy, vine-ripened tomatoes.

"That's cold."

"Complain, complain," I said. A sandwich ain't a sandwich without olives. Or green peppers. Next something spicy. When I mentioned jalapenos, he just about jumped from the table.

"Fuck that!" he yelled.

"All right, all right. Nothing hot." I added a dash of salt. No pepper. "Eat your fuckin' heart out, Picasso."

"Are you done?" he asked, "'cause my legs are starting to fall asleep."

I pulled off the gloves and shoved them in the metal trough beneath the cutting board.

I was tempted to just ram my face into his scrumptious butt, piggish and messy. Armando shifted anxiously. My dick was dripping in anticipation of the feast to come. He had never looked more delicious. His ass was so pretty I didn't want to touch it. But I couldn't hold back. I pulled at his thighs, opening him up as I began to chew. He heaved and sighed as I ate. I was a mess, but I didn't give a shit. I pressed him into the table, occasionally nipping his ass with bites of love. My appetite was insatiable. He was an all-you-can-eat buffet of manliness. When I was done, his ass was littered with bits of olives, pieces of tomato, scraps of meat and streaks of mustard. Armando was a nasty, naked beautiful sight.

"I can't eat another bite."

Armando eased his legs off the cutting board. He sat up and stretched happily, still hard but hardly satisfied. I went back to sucking him off. Armando ran his dickhead over my lips, across the rug of my tongue.

"Ready for some dessert?" he asked. He cocked his legs on my shoulders as I uncorked his dick out of my mouth. The left-over mayonnaise was slick on my dick. I slid myself into his ass. I hugged Armando's thighs as I pressed and pushed. Tears of sweat beaded his taut stomach. He whacked off as I thrust into him. He spoke dirty to me in Italian. Armando's face was flushed. I couldn't hold back. I slid out of my baby and came across his stomach. Armando came seconds after me. I rubbed my cum into his chest and tongued the last few droplets into my mouth.

We sat, flesh touching flesh and sweat mixing with sweat, hearts still pounding.

I'd be so glad when we got our own crib, when we didn't have to meet behind closed blinds and locked doors.

"I'll help yuh clean up," I said, exhausted. I grabbed a wet cloth from the kitchen sink and wiped off Armando and myself the best I could. Every muscle ached as we pulled on our pants, worked our arms through the sleeves of our shirts. Armando finished stacking the chairs and mopping, while I cleaned the food area of the store and the kitchen.

"Anything else I can do?"

"Just go home and pack," he said, kissing me good night. I didn't want to let go. I wanted to hold him, breathe in his sandwich shop scent of pepperoni and mustard.

I was worried about getting caught when I got home, but I was excited because I would soon be leaving the evil castle on Charlie Ash Lane. I killed the headlights and the engine in the road, put the car in NEUTRAL and pushed it quietly the rest of the way into the driveway. I climbed carefully back through the window, but just as I climbed into bed, lights blazed on. There she was: Ma, with anger in her eyes.

"Boy, where you been?" she asked.

"Jus' up th' street."

"You a lie!" she hollered. "You went to go see that boy didn't you?"

I thought of Armando and what he would do if he were here. He'd stand up to her. I took my beating in stride, with pride and strength, because with Armando in my heart, I could feel no pain.

ABOUT THE
AUTHORS

JONATHAN ASCHE's work has appeared in numerous anthologies, including *Rough Trade* and *Muscle Men*. He is also the author of the erotic novels *Mindjacker* and *Money Shots,* as well as *Kept Men and Other Erotic Stories*. He lives in Atlanta with his husband, Tome.

R. J. BRADSHAW currently resides in Saskatoon, Saskatchewan, where he founded a romantic greeting card company to showcase his poetry. His short fiction has been published by Cleis Press, Queered Fiction and Starbooks Press.

NATHAN BURGOINE lives in Ottawa, Canada. His previous erotic works can be found in *I Like it Like That*, *Tented* and *Blood Sacraments*. You can find him online at n8an.livejournal. com. His silver line ends at his husband, Daniel.

RACHEL KRAMER BUSSEL (rachelkramerbussel.com) is

a New York–based author, editor and blogger. She is senior editor at *Penthouse Variations* and hosts In the Flesh Reading Series. Her books include *Crossdressing, The Mile High Club, Bottoms Up, Spanked, Peep Show, Tasting Him, Do Not Disturb* and more.

HEIDI CHAMPA has been published in numerous anthologies including *College Boys, Like Magnets We Attract, Skater Boys* and *Hard Working Men*. Short stories can also be found at Dreamspinner Press, Ravenous Romance and Torquere Press. Find more online at heidichampa.blogspot.com.

HANK EDWARDS is the author of several erotic novels, including *Fluffers, Inc., A Carnal Cruise* and *Vancouver Nights*, as well as *Holed Up* and *Destiny's Bastard*. He and his partner live in a suburb of Detroit. Visit his website at hankedwardsbooks.com.

PEPPER ESPINOZA has published erotic romance novels with Amber Heat, Amber Allure, Samhain, Loose Id and Liquid Silver Books. Writing as Jamie Craig, she also has books placed with all the aforementioned publishers as well as MLR Press and Carina Books. For a complete listing of her novels and novellas, please visit pepperverse.net.

D. FOSTALOVE lives in Atlanta, Georgia, where he is currently at work on several projects, including a follow-up to *Unraveled: Sealed Lips, Clenched Fists*.

KYLE LUKOFF is a writer and aspiring librarian living in Brooklyn, New York. He has been published in many anthologies, including *Gender Outlaws, I Like It Like That* and *Girl Crazy*.

JEFF MANN's books include *Bones Washed with Wine* and *On the Tongue* (poetry); *Edge: Travels of an Appalachian Leather Bear; Devoured* (a novella); *Loving Mountains, Loving Men* and *A History of Barbed Wire*, winner of a Lambda Literary Award. He teaches creative writing at Virginia Tech in Blacksburg, Virginia.

GREGORY L. NORRIS is a full-time professional writer with work routinely published in national magazines and fiction anthologies. He is the author of the handbook to all-things-Sunnydale, *The Q Guide to Buffy the Vampire Slayer*. Norris lives at and writes from the outer limits of New Hampshire.

STEPHEN OSBORNE has had stories published in *Backdraft, Best Gay Love Stories 2010, Unmasked I* and *II, Nerdvana, Queer Wolf and Best Gay Love Stories: Summer Flings*. He is also the author of *South Bend Ghosts and Other Northern Indiana Haunts*. He can be followed on Twitter under the moniker southbendghosts.

JAY ROGERS lives with his blue collar husband in the heart of Iowa. He works as a software specialist in the healthcare industry.

ROB ROSEN, author of the novels *Sparkle: The Queerest Book You'll Ever Love* and *Divas Las Vegas,* has contributed to *Best Gay Romance (2007, 2008, 2009, & 2010),* several volumes of *Best Gay Love Stories, Backdraft, Surfer Boys, Special Forces* and *Ultimate Gay Erotica 2008 & 2009.* Contact: therobrosen.com.

BOB VICKERY is the author of *Cock Tales, Play Buddies* and *Cocksure: Erotic Fiction*.

LOGAN ZACHARY's stories can be found in *Hard Hats, Taken By Force, Boys Caught in the Act, Ride Me Cowboy, Best Gay Erotica 2009, Ultimate Gay Erotica 2009, Surfer Boys, Sextime, Queer Dimensions, Obsessed, College Boys, Teammates, Homo Thugs, Black Fire, Skater Boys, Men At Noon, Monsters At Midnight* and *Rough Trade*. Contact: LoganZachary2002@yahoo.com.

ABOUT
THE EDITOR

SHANE ALLISON is the proud editor of *Hot Cops: Gay Erotic Stories, Backdraft: Fireman Erotica, College Boys: Gay Erotic Stories,* and *Hard Working Men: Gay Erotic Stories.* His stories have appeared in *Best Black Gay Erotica,* five editions of *Best Gay Erotica, Bears, Biker Boys, Leathermen, Surfer Boys, Country Boys* and over a dozen other lusty anthologies. His first book of poems, *Slut Machine* is out from Rebel Satori Press. Shane currently lives in Tallahassee, Florida. He would like to thank everyone at Cleis Press for their tireless work in bringing this and other anthologies to life.

More Gay Erotic Stories from Shane Allison

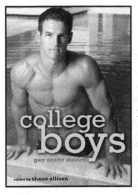

College Boys
Gay Erotic Stories
Edited by Shane Allison

First feelings of lust for another boy, all-night study sessions, the excitement of a student hot for a teacher...is it any wonder that college boys are the objects of fantasy the world over?
ISBN 978-1-57344-399-9 $14.95

Hot Cops
Gay Erotic Stories
Edited by Shane Allison

"From smooth and fit to big and hairy... it's like a downtown locker room where everyone has some sort of badge."—*Bay Area Reporter*
ISBN 978-1-57344-277-0 $14.95

Backdraft
Fireman Erotica
Edited by Shane Allison

"Seriously: This book is so scorching hot that you should box it with a fire extinguisher and ointment. It will burn more than your fingers." —*Tucson Weekly*
ISBN 978-1-57344-325-8 $14.95

More of the Very Best from Cleis Press

Best Gay Erotica 2010
Edited by Richard Labonté
Selected and introduced by Blair Mastbaum
ISBN 978-1-57344-374-6 $15.95

Skater Boys
Gay Erotic Stories
Edited by Neil Plakcy
ISBN 978-1-57344-401-9 $14.95

Best of the Best Gay Erotica 3
Edited by Richard Labonté
ISBN 978-1-57344-410-1 $14.95

A Sticky End
A Mitch Mitchell Mystery
By James Lear
ISBN 978-1-57344-395-1 $14.95

Ordering is easy! Call us toll free or fax us to place your MC/VISA order.
You can also mail the order form below with payment to:
Cleis Press, 2246 Sixth St., Berkeley, CA 94710.

ORDER FORM

QTY	TITLE	PRICE
	SUBTOTAL	
	SHIPPING	
	SALES TAX	
	TOTAL	

Add $3.95 postage/handling for the first book ordered and $1.00 for each additional book. Outside North America, please contact us for shipping rates. California residents add 9.75% sales tax. Payment in U.S. dollars only.

★ **Free book of equal or lesser value. Shipping and applicable sales tax extra.**

Cleis Press • Phone: (800) 780-2279 • Fax: 510-845-8001
orders@cleispress.com • www.cleispress.com
You'll find more great books on our website

Follow us on Twitter @cleispress • Friend/fan us on Facebook